THE EGYPTIAN FALCON

Iain McLaughlin

Erimem: The Egyptian Falcon © Iain McLaughlin
Editor: Julianne Todd
Range Editor: Iain McLaughlin
First published in 2018
Erimem and associated concepts Copyright © 2018 Iain McLaughlin
All rights reserved.
Cover illustration by Grace Prentis
Warrior Queen of the Nile Poster and Publicity photo by Dorina Petco
No part of this publication may be reproduced, stored in a retrieval system or
transmitted in any form or by any means, electronic, mechanical, photocopying,
recording or any other manner without prior written permission of the copyright
holder.
First published in 2018 by Thebes Publishing
follow us online:
www.thebespublishing.com
https://www.facebook.com/ThebesPublishing
https://twitter.com/ThebesNews
ISBN: 978-1-910868-32-4

THEBES PUBLISHING

ERIMEM

THE EGYPTIAN FALCON

CHAPTER ONE

Cleary's Bar is in the wrong town.

It's the most *Irish* Irish Bar I ever saw.

It's an Irish bar selling Irish stout and Irish whiskey and Irish clichés. You don't have to be Irish to buy any of it.

Cleary was full-on Irish himself. I'll give him that. He'd been run out of Dublin in his late teens around the turn of the century. He had the choice – run as far as he could or face an angry father with a shotgun and the prospect of a life of diapers. He ran and didn't stop running till he got to New York. His Irish bar there did good business until Prohibition started. Hell, he did good business well *after* Prohibition started. It was only when some cops he couldn't buy off found out about it that Cleary had to start running again. He made his way to California in the mid-Twenties and he's bitched about the sun and heat here ever since.

Cleary is one miserable Irish son-of-a-bitch.

It's one of the reasons I go to his bar. He owns successful restaurants. He somehow makes an Irish bar that belongs in New York work here in LA. Hell, the ugly son-of-a-bitch one way or another even got himself a gorgeous wife. She's twenty years younger than him and could have done much better for herself. And he still complains. You don't get that kind of honesty much in this town. That's why I come here.

That and the fact that it's the best place around to pick up information. You can pick up other things as well if you're not careful. I knew a guy who came in here for a drink and left with a wife. It was his bad luck to be drinking here when a judge was in. Another fella had worse luck a year later. He picked up something nasty from one of the girls working her trade here and his wife did some home-style dental work with a frying pan.

I'd always been more careful than that. For one thing, I never let a broad get heavy with me. Not after... not after last time. For another, I never mixed business and pleasure. Sure, I liked Cleary and his bar but I only went there for work.

I'm a Seamus. A damned good one, too. I was a better cop, but that's ancient history. A bullet in the leg and a captain in the pocket of the no-good mook who put the bullet there persuaded me to take them up on retirement when it was offered. I guess they didn't have to pension me off. I should be grateful they didn't just shoot me in the face and dump me in the Pacific. I wouldn't have been the first. Sure as Hell wouldn't have been the last either.

A cop's pension doesn't go far these days and the pay-out I got only just paid the bar tab from the retirement party. So I went from police detective to private detective. A PI. One week I was chasing murderers, the next I was taking pictures of wives testing the bedsprings with somebody who wasn't their old man or snapping a cheating husband playing hide-the-weenie with his secretary. And the secretary was always too young for the old bum. Too young, too pretty and usually too scared of losing her job to say no.

And I took pictures as evidence.

It paid the bills but it ate the soul.

Some days the mirror made for tough viewing.

I was lucky. This visit I was making to Cleary's was for a case that might actually have had some real investigating.

Some real money, too.

I was meeting some guy named Gray. I didn't know anything about him except the name. That's not unusual in this game. Everybody keeps secrets.

Mr Gray.

I'd never seen him before but it didn't need to be Basil Rathbone to work out that the guy sitting in the furthest away booth was Gray. It wasn't just his name. Everything about the poor schlub was gray. His hair was gray, so were his suit, the hat he'd put on the table, his eyes, even his complexion. Let me tell you, in this city you don't meet too many people who hide from the sun like this guy.

'Mr Gray?' I said. Well, it paid to ask.

He looked up at me, no interest at all in those dull eyes. No life either. 'Mr Stone, I assume.'

Jeez, even his voice was gray.

I slid into the booth and sat opposite the gray man. There was something about the guy I just didn't take to so I got straight to business. Better to know if I was going to take his money or not. 'Mitchell Stone,' I agreed. 'What can I do for you, Mr Gray?'

Gray hardly moved. I had to pinch myself to stay awake while his monotone voice was talking. 'I believe you have a good reputation in your field, Mr Stone.'

'I like to think so,' I answered.

'You have many connections left over from your time in the police force.'

Was that a question or a statement? I couldn't tell. I just agreed. 'I do.'

'And contacts in the moving picture industry.'

Jeez, this guy really wasn't from LA. Nobody here had time to call the movies anything as long winded as "the moving picture industry".

As it turns out he was right. I did have some contacts in the movies. I'd done some work for a producer whose wife had been getting some fun away from home. He had thought she was testing bedsprings with some guy at a health spa. Turned out she *was* cheating but she liked getting her kicks with other chicks. It also turned out that hubby didn't have a problem with that. From what I hear he butters his bread on both sides as well. As long as she only plays away with other dames, he doesn't mind. So they're still married. But I was discreet and I kept everything on the low-down so he sent more work my way. If things went missing in Hollywood, I got the call. Hell, if *people* went missing in Hollywood, I got the call. A couple of the guys I was on the Force with started calling me the Hollywood Dick and the Showbiz Seamus. None of it was meant as a compliment.

'Yeah,' I told Gray. 'I know my way around Tinseltown. You got some kind of problem in there?'

'Not a problem,' he answered. 'Someone working in your...

Hollywood simply purchased an artefact which rightly belonged to me.'

'Yeah?' That sounded like a line if ever I heard one. This town was full of stories of people with sticky fingers helping themselves to other people's property. That included other people's husbands and wives. I guessed this Gray wasn't interested in anybody's bedtime activities. Not even his own. 'You're gonna have to give me more information than that,' I told him. 'I need details. What's the item you're talking about? Why was it yours? How did somebody else come to have it?' I glanced over towards the bar and nodded at Cleary. He knew what it meant. He knew what I drank. 'I need info, Mr Gray.'

Gray looked at me. I've been stared at by some of the meanest sons-of-bitches in this town. Been slugged by some of them too. This guy's dead eyes were way more disturbing than any of them. At least I knew what they were thinking. I couldn't tell with this one.

'Here.' Cleary put a healthy slug of bourbon on the table in front of me.

I thanked him but Cleary was already on his way back to the bar. He knew better than to hang around when business was being done.

I took a belt of the bourbon. My first of the day. 'So?' I pushed Gray. 'You going to give me the details or do I finish my drink and walk?'

Those damn eyes didn't flicker. 'Very well,' he said. 'I am a dealer in antiquities. Some I gather for museums and exhibitions, others I procure for private collectors.'

He was lying. I could tell. It didn't matter. Not yet anyway. I pushed him. 'And this was for?'

'None of your business.' The voice hadn't changed tone.

So why did I feel a chill when he spoke?

'Fair enough,' I said. 'I still need details.'

Gray took a second before he answered. 'There is an importer I work with... *worked with*,' he corrected. I didn't like the sound of that switch to the past tense. 'He imported objects for me. I was not his only patron. Unfortunately for him he accidentally passed the piece to another of his clients, a small antiques shop. They, in turn, sold it on to one of their customers.'

'I hope that wasn't unfortunate for the shop's owner,' I said. There was a bit of threat in my voice I hadn't expected.

'They were not at fault,' Gray said, 'and they willingly provided the details of their customer.'

'Under duress?' I asked.

'There was no need,' Gray said. 'They appreciate the value of money.'

'Doesn't everybody?' Yeah, that was a hint.

Gray picked up on it. He reached into his pocket and slid an envelope across the table. I opened it and looked inside. I guessed there were twenty five ten dollar bills in there. I have an eye for that kind of guessing.

'I assume that is enough?' Gray said.

Two hundred and fifty bucks? That was more than enough to cover me for two months. Adding my pension, I would be on easy street through the summer. I might even manage to take a few days' vacation.

I still played it cagey and left the envelope on the table. *My side* of the table, obviously, but still in view. 'I guess you want this thing pretty bad, huh?'

'If that isn't enough I will pay the same again when you deliver the artefact to me.'

Five hundred bucks. Well, that confirmed that this S.O.B. was up to his ass in illegal business. You know what? For five hundred bucks I didn't care.

'Okay,' I told Gray, 'but for double this. Five hundred. Now what is it you want me to get back for you and who in Hollywood bought it?'

Gray pulled a photograph from his pocket and slid it across the table. In the picture was a statue. What looked like one of those hawk artefacts they found in Egyptian tombs twenty years back was resting on a newspaper printed in some kind of Arabic language. 'An Egyptian Falcon,' Gray said.

'Genuine?' I asked.

'Of course. There is no profit for forgeries.' He tapped the photograph. 'This was bought from the antique shop for the sum of one dollar by a young woman named Lisa Borden who works for Centurion Studios. It seems that her employers are soon to begin filming a motion picture set in ancient Egypt and Miss

Borden is one of those whose task is to make the... I believe they call it "the set"... her task is to make "the set" look genuine. That is why she bought the Falcon.'

That all sounded plausible and way too simple. 'I'm gonna guess there's a reason you don't just take a cab over to Centurion's studios and buy the piece back from Miss Borden? I estimate that would save you roughly four hundred ninety eight bucks and some change.'

He didn't answer.

'Okay,' I carried on. 'I also guess you want your name kept out of things when I do this.'

'That is correct, Mr Stone.'

'Fair enough,' I agreed. 'I got a reputation for discretion.'

'Good,' Gray said. He slid – oozed is probably closer to the truth - along the seat and stood. 'One more thing, Mr Stone. There will be other people interested in acquiring the artefact.'

I felt that sick feeling in my gut. He'd saved the worst for last. I knew it wasn't going to be good. 'Who else wants it?' I asked. 'Who's after it?'

'Some European collectors.' That was pretty much it. He told me I should only call him when I had the bird. 'I don't expect to hear from you before then. Nor do I expect to hear from anyone else about this.'

You know, the slimy little weasel even walked in a gray way. Short steps. He hardly looked like he was touching the ground at all. I swear the bar got warmer the minute the door closed behind him. The damn place looker brighter, too.

I slipped the envelope and the photograph of the bird into the inside pocket of my jacket.

Cleary was back at my table. 'You want another?'

'Yeah,' I answered automatically. When Cleary offers the good stuff it's damn near impossible to refuse. On the other hand, when somebody offers five hundred bucks for the easiest job I had all year, I should at least stay sober while I do it. 'Change of plan,' I told Cleary. 'A cup of that dishwater you call coffee. Then I need to get my ass to work.'

CHAPTER TWO

You make odd discoveries when your best friend is a time-travelling Pharaoh from Egypt's Middle Kingdom, about three and a half thousand years ago. One of those things is that most of my pop culture references fly straight over her head. *Whoosh!* I let loose what I think is a zinger and she looks at me blankly or as if I've just said the stupidest thing she's ever heard. But she remembers stuff. Sometimes I think she remembers *everything*. If I make a comment she might laugh at it six months later when she finally sees what it was actually about. The first time I met her we saw Cleopatra. Yes, *that* Cleopatra. At some point I did an "Infamy, infamy" gag. Eight months later she finally saw *Carry On Cleo* and she damn near wet herself laughing. It wasn't just that the film is funny – and it really is and I will punch anybody who disagrees – she kept laughing at how far from the real Cleopatra and Antony the film versions were. That's another interesting thing about time travel. We get to meet historical figures and compare them to how history and Hollywood have portrayed them. Some, like Cleopatra, just aren't what we expect them to be. Others, like Elvis Presley, do not disappoint. I didn't get it with his movies but when I met him on a trip to 1961? He could have turned me straight if he'd tried. He didn't try, though. I'm not sure if I was disappointed or not. He really was a gentleman.

Erimem and I had been out to see a movie. The latest *Marvel* film. We'd already seen it in the future but seeing it on the big screen in plain old 3D is a bit special.

We stopped off on the way back to Erimem's place to get chips. Well, I say "Erimem's place". What I mean is the upstairs airing cupboard in Ibrahim and Helena's house. It's not actually a cupboard. It's a portal into an artificial dimension which is currently programmed to look like a kind of Egyptian villa. That's Erimem's place. Bet you're sorry you asked. I had to get her to read – well, watch – *Harry Potter* and *Narnia* stories so she'd understand how I described it.

We got back to the house around eleven. Ibrahim and Helena still haven't been married that long. They fancied a quiet night in watching an old movie – which I think is newlywed code for something else – so we gave them the house for the night so they could watch their film and do whatever else they felt like. Being that we are nice people we also picked up chips for Ibrahim and Helena.

The pair of them had a strange look on their faces when we got in.

'Good film?' Ibrahim asked. It was a simple question but he had managed to make it sound really pointed.

Erimem had picked up on it, too. 'Yes, is there a reason it wouldn't be?' She sounded puzzled.

'No, no,' Ibrahim said. 'No reason.'

'We just thought you might like an older film,' Helena chipped in. Jesus, she was in on the pointed statements, too. It wasn't like her.

'No,' Erimem answered slowly. 'We told you which film we were going to see.'

'We know,' Helena nodded.

Ibrahim took over. 'But we thought you might have gone to see an old movie...' he turned to Helena. 'Like that one we saw tonight. What was it called?'

Helena nodded eagerly and overplayed her part just too much. 'Just what I was thinking. It was called *Warrior Queen of the Nile*, wasn't it?'

'The very one.' Christ, Ibrahim had moved into ad-dram performance now.

'Okay,' I said. 'You two clearly have a bee up your arses about something. Spill the beans.'

'Yes,' Erimem agreed. 'Tell us or we will not let you have

your chips.'

Helena scowled. 'Do you really think we'll cave under the threat of not getting our chips?'

'*You* will not,' Erimem shook her head, 'but Ibrahim will. We got curry sauce with his.'

Ibrahim shrugged in resignation. 'Okay, curry sauce wins,' he said, nodding towards the sitting room door. 'Sit down. We've got something to show you.'

We were curious, so did as we were told. We sat on the couch and Ibrahim aimed the remote at the TV. A second later the opening of a creaky old black and white movie flickered up on the screen.

The title card was a white on black Art Deco representation of a Roman Centurion in full uniform. As soon as that faded we were into a really ropey bit of theme music. It had that reedy thin sound some 1930s and 40s movies had. A stylised card came up. Pyramids, hieroglyphs and a list of performers. I didn't recognise any of the names to be honest.

JOHN BUTTLER
PETER ARTHUR
CLEMENTINE REED
RICHARD FLEMING
ELENA ORTEGA

And then a second card flashed up.

'Oh,' Erimem said. 'I didn't expect that.'

'Me either,' I said quietly.

and introducing
ERIMEM SMITH as
the WARRIOR QUEEN OF THE NILE

'Maybe it's not you...' I knew how lame that sounded. 'I mean, you've never been to Hollywood...'

'Never,' Erimem agreed. 'Probably.'

The picture on the screen changed. The cards ran through technicians, writers and producers and finished on

Directed by
CARSON REED

None of us were paying attention to the director's name. We were all looking at the woman in the background. In flickering old black and white, dressed in Hollywood's take on Egyptian clothing, *khopesh* blades in her hands, was Erimem.

'No?' I asked. 'She certainly looks familiar.'

'It is definitely me,' Erimem said. She stood up and crossed to the screen. She peered intently at her image. 'And I look *good*.'

'Shrink your head a bit,' I told her. 'The screen's only fifty inches.'

Erimem glanced at Ibrahim. 'Am I in this movie a lot?'

He nodded. 'Oh, yeah.'

'You're the star,' Helena added. 'Well, as much as anyone who wasn't white was allowed to be the star.'

Erimem snorted. 'That is stupid.'

Helena nodded. 'But true.'

Ibrahim agreed. 'We were usually either the villains or some untrustworthy cheat or at best the hero's sidekick...'

'...who was usually either comic relief or met a plucky but painful end,' Helena finished for him. They had got to the point of completing each other's sentences. It was either cute or sickening. I couldn't decide which.

Ibrahim had become a bit more serious. 'It really is unusual for somebody of colour to have such a prominent role.'

'What kind of part is it?' Erimem asked curiously.

I said, 'I'd say the title's a bit of a giveaway.'

Erimem waved my interruption away. 'But is she a hero or a villain?' she asked.

Ibrahim scowled. 'You want me to give away the ending?'

'Just tell me.'

'Well,' Ibrahim began, 'she starts as a shadowy figure who...'

Helena cut to the chase. '... who travels through time against her will from Pharaoh's palace to modern London.'

'London, my arse,' Ibrahim snorted.

'Hollywood's version of London,' Helena conceded. 'Where she fights off the spirit of an evil Egyptian priest who wants to inhabit a handsome young chap's body.'

'And ravish his girlfriend,' Ibrahim added.

Helena nodded. 'At least as much as they did ravish anybody in the movies in the Forties. One foot on the floor for decency's sake and all that.'

'Sounds better than Tom Cruise's Mummy film,' I muttered.

Erimem turned slowly and gave me *that* look. 'You didn't watch it.'

That was true. We gave up after twenty minutes. 'Neither did you.'

Helena was keen to get back on topic. 'So when did you make this film?' she asked Erimem.

Erimem just shrugged. 'I don't know. Obviously I haven't done it yet.'

A thought struck me. 'Oh, god.'

'What?' Erimem frowned.

'You'll have an IMDB page,' I said. She looked at me blankly. 'A page?' I explained. 'A page on the internet.'

Erimem snorted in annoyance. 'I am supposed to be living here quietly.'

It wasn't that big of a deal really. Was it? 'Don't worry,' I told her. 'We'll fix it so she's a distant relative you look remarkably like. Make that *another* distant relative you look remarkably like.' We had already used that excuse a couple of times.

Helena opened her chips and started eating. 'Maybe if you just don't go back and don't make that film we can avoid this happening.'

'Problem solved,' Ibrahim agreed, also opening his chips. 'You really did get curry sauce. Thanks.'

Erimem shook her head firmly. 'I do not think so.' She was staring at the screen. 'We *must* go to Hollywood in 1940.'

I almost laughed. 'Oh, come on. You can't be that keen to be a movie star. I admit it might be cool....'

Erimem ignored me. She was pointing at the screen. 'Freeze the picture. There. Do you see this?'

I followed her finger. 'A little bird?'

'A statue?' Ibrahim suggested.

Erimem nodded. She was serious. The kind of serious that usually meant trouble. 'That is a rare relic, held by the Pharaohs of the Two Kingdoms as part of the secret rites which protect us and hold evil in check.'

That sounded like mumbo-jumbo to me. 'You don't believe that.'

'It *might* also be able to raise the dead,' Erimem answered.

She wasn't joking.

'Might?' I asked. 'You don't remember?'

She frowned and her brow furrowed. 'There were many artefacts and I cannot remember *everything* about *all* of them.'

'But you remember that one,' Helena said, munching on a chip.

'Oh, yes,' Erimem agreed. 'Shemek, the priest, warned me not to be misled by how small and ordinary it looks. Its power is enormous.'

'It could be a copy,' I said reasonably. 'How can you tell it's real?'

'Can you rewind the film?' Erimem said to Ibrahim.

'Of course,' Ibrahim said. He stopped and scowled. 'And how do you know about rewinding? Videos were obsolete years before you arrived.'

She wasn't paying attention. The statue was large enough for us to see the pictographs on a little plinth under the statue. 'Stop. There. Can you read the hieroglyphs?'

'No,' Ibrahim squinted at the screen. 'I'm a bit rusty. Let me see...'

'No need,' Erimem said. 'I recognise the inscription and the dialect.' She nodded to herself. 'The statue is real.'

'That's could be somebody on the art team being way too clever,' I argued.

Erimem pointed at an inscription beside the statue. 'Or I remembered seeing this message and when I go back in time I have it put there so that I would read it now.'

Ibrahim squinted. 'It says "Erimem this is real", I think.'

'It does,' Erimem confirmed. 'And it is signed – by me.'

I shrugged and nodded. She had persuaded me. 'Aren't you a sneaky bugger?'

'Apparently I am a *very* sneaky bugger.' She glanced back at the screen appreciatively. 'And those clothes might be all wrong but I look *really* good in them.'

You know what was annoying? She was right. She did.

We didn't actually go to Hollywood straight away. The first thing we did was watch the film. You know something? It wasn't bad. It wasn't great either, but I've seen worse. As for Erimem... well, she didn't have much *acting* to do. Most of her scenes were basically fighting and she's always been good at kicking the crap out of people. It really took me ages to get used to seeing her on the screen in black and white... while she was sitting next to me in living, chip-munching colour. But I got used to it. That's life, really, isn't it? No matter what changes get stuck in front of you, you deal with them and you get used to them.

So, my friend, the uncrowned Pharaoh of all Egypt from three millennia ago, was also a movie star from Hollywood's Golden Age. And how many people have actually used that sentence? I mean... how many people have used that sentence *ever*?

So we watched the movie and then went online to find out about the film. One of the first things we found after a really unhelpful and snarky Wiki page was an interview with the director Carson Reed saying where and when he had discovered Erimem. That told us where and when we needed to be. None of us were working the next day so we had a good night's sleep before gathering in Erimem's villa. We'd all dressed in clothes appropriate for the period and packed clothes for various eventualities. Some were everyday, some really swanky. One of the great things about Erimem's apartment is that it can rustle up clothes for any situation. Good thing – I never have to pay a fortune for really nice clothes. Bad thing – sometimes the clothes are too precise and accurate for the time. 1940's underwear, for example... the knickers are so big you could go camping in them. As for the bras, they just heaved everything in and pointed it forward. Back support? Comfort? Forget it. Just point those things like we're all Fembots or old school Madonna. Helena seemed okay with the clothes, but sometimes I do forget that she's worn these clothes before. She's almost two and a half thousand years old so whatever clothes we find, she's probably worn them before.

And looked great in them.

She makes *everything* look good.

Makes you sick, sometimes.

I have to say, we all did look rather good, despite being heaved in all directions by our undercrackers.

'Is everyone prepared?' Erimem asked.

'Are *you* ready?' Helena asked Erimem.

'Me?' Erimem looked bemused. 'What do I need to prepare for?'

'Hollywood,' Helena answered.

'It is just people making silly films,' Erimem snorted. 'How dangerous can that be?'

We put on the time travel rings and I programmed our destination into the transportation system. A few seconds later, there we were in Hollywood in 1940. To be accurate, there we were in an alley in downtown Los Angeles in late summer, 1940. We knew we'd hit our dates from a discarded newspaper. We made our way out of the alley onto a street.

'Bloody hell, we really *are* in Hollywood.' I am nothing if not classy. You can take me anywhere. You just can't take me there twice.

It was like we were in an old movie. Everybody had the clothes, the look. The cars were those old automobiles you see in old black and white films. The traffic was pretty light, too. The sun was beating down. It was *incredibly* hot.

We had arrived in a pretty well to-do part of town. According to a clock in a shop window – nope, let's make that a *store* window – it was just coming up to half past eleven in the morning. According to the interview we had read, Erimem Smith lived in a house in Beverly Hills. We saw an estate agent – I can't be arsed calling them a realtor, it's a stupid word – and looked through the properties they had on offer. They were sniffy about renting us a house. Oh, yeah, you can bet your arse that was everything to do with Erimem and Ibrahim's race. However, we dropped into conversation that Erimem was an actress and was to make a movie. Suddenly they couldn't do enough for us. The fact that Erimem's Habitat had rattled up a shit ton of cash didn't hurt either. They offered us a couple of places which we turned down. They didn't sound like the house the director had mentioned. The third one was on the money though and we were taken to see it straight away. It's amazing how much they'll do for you in Hollywood when you have cash.

As soon as we saw the house we all knew it was the place

that had been mentioned in the interview. It was in a very comfortable part of Beverly Hills but it wasn't exactly showbiz central. It was a big, detached house with a good size garden and a nice little pool. There were five bedrooms and the whole thing was light and bright. I really liked it. We agreed to rent it on the spot, even though it was *hellishly* expensive.

We moved in immediately. Our estate agent, a real slimer by the name of Pendew, arranged for us to have a car and a maid. He was surprised we didn't want a cook and a driver. We didn't care. Having a maid was bad enough. I admit I felt guilty about us hiring somebody – presumably a woman – when we'd only be there a few weeks tops. Helena felt the same way.

'We'll leave her a really good bonus when we go,' she said.

Helena and I went out and did our grocery shopping. Neither Ibrahim nor Erimem were all that interested so just the two of us went. It was a bit of a shock to the likes of me who was used to buying everything pre-packaged from a supermarket. Everything was fresh and bought loose or from a specialist. I kind of enjoyed it. I'm absolutely certain Helena loved it.

'No plastic wrapping,' was all she said, but she was obviously enjoying herself.

When we got back to the house, most of the doors and windows were open, airing the place. While Ibrahim had done that Erimem had scouted the house, working out if there was a weak point in the house or its grounds. Quite what she was expecting, I don't know. Hordes of aggressive autograph hunters? Errol Flynn trying to get up her trellis? Now there's a *Carry On* line for you. From what I'd heard of Errol Flynn, though... yeah, probably best to know what was what when it came to protecting the place. I suppose it was a wealthy sort of area, so burglars were a possibility. Yeah, she was definitely right to have checked it all out.

We were settled in by six o'clock and ate out by the pool. We'd all changed into swimming costumes. I can't call what Helena, Erimem and I wore bikinis. They barely showed any midriff. I suppose they were daring for the time. This wasn't the time or place for flashing the flesh. So, no topless sunbathing here.

Even so, sitting out there on the terrace, eating the salad I'd prepared with Helena, while soaking up the California sun, I actually did feel like we were going Hollywood.

And I liked it.

CHAPTER THREE

This should have been the easiest job of my life.

All I had to do was go to the studio, schmooze some chick and get the statue back for Mr Dull. If I was quick, whoever else was interested would still be eating lunch while I was handing the bird over and counting the Ben Franklins.

Yeah, this should have been the easiest job of my life.

Should have been.

Could have been.

But it wasn't.

I drove to Centurion Studios. They weren't the biggest players in Hollywood. They didn't make the biggest movies or have the top stars on their books but their picture did okay. They were the kind of movies that killed an hour and a half or that a guy might take a date to if they weren't planning to focus on the picture, if you get my drift. A double feature from Centurion was a couple of hours' solid smooching time.

They made some good pictures too. They churned out three or four of those sentimental *Billy Dolan* flicks every year. I guess they were on to their fourth Billy by now. Every time he looked too old for high school they canned the schlub and replaced him with the next freckled face on the assembly line. That's the movies for ya, kid. I didn't like the *Billy Dolan* pictures but they made money. Their westerns and their cop movies were more my kind of thing. Jake Ford was their big star. He had the tag of being the cut-price John Wayne. There was some truth in that. He looked kinda like Wayne. The same height and kinda craggy look. And the truth was that if somebody took an idea for a picture for Wayne to Republic and they turned it down, chances are it got made at Centurion with Jake Ford only on a quarter of the budget. Give him a decent director and something worth saying, Ford was a pretty decent actor. Pity for him, so was Wayne. I saw *Stagecoach* a few times when it came out in '39. He was good in that. They say Wayne's going to be really big. Hell, I knew that when I saw *Born to the West* a few years ago.

I guess Centurion's other big name was William Taylor. *Tough guy Bill Taylor* turned up in most of their better cop or private eye pictures. I met him a few times and gave him some tips on how we operate. He was a hell of an actor. Hated violence, couldn't stand guns but made his living shooting bad guys, feeding knuckles to snitches and kissing the dames. Yeah, that last bit was acting for him too. Who cares? He was a good guy, that's what mattered.

Centurion Studios weren't exactly subtle with the décor at their gates. A twelve foot high statue of a Roman Centurion stood on either side of the entrance. I think they were probably plaster rather than stone. They still had more range of expression than some of the actors in this town.

Miguel Rodriguez was on duty at the gate. He remembered me from my previous visits to the studio. 'Hi, Mr Stone. You got an appointment?'

'Something like that,' I answered cagily.

In my game we always answer cagily.

Miguel looked at the sheet of paper on top of his clipboard. 'Nobody put you on the list, Mr Stone.'

I leaned closer, all conspiratorial. 'And that's how they'd like to keep it.' I nodded for emphasis. 'If you get my drift?'

Miguel nodded. He got it all right. A stream of BS and he bought it all. 'Same as first time, huh?'

I gave him a knowing half-grin. 'Something like that.'

'Same client?'

I tilted my head and gave him a look. 'If I tell ya, it won't be confidential any more, will it, Miguel?' *Wait a second, wait a second. Reel him in.* 'I ain't saying you're right, Miguel.' I shrugged. 'But I sure ain't saying you're wrong either.'

I'd told him absolutely nothing. He thought I'd told him everything. That suited us both. He waved me in through the gates and I drove to the parking lot. I parked in a nice, quiet place. The fewer people who knew I there the happier I was.

Mr Dull-Gray said Lisa Borden had bought the bird to use on an Egyptian movie. That meant she worked as a set dresser in the Set Decoration department. I remembered where that was from the times I'd been to the studio before.

Centurion had eight studio stages. They looked like big warehouses. Each one was marked by the Centurion logo and a number from one to eight picked out in Roman numerals. It looked like they had westerns going in one and four, and a crime flick in two. From the white tie and tails of the guys going in and out, some kind of lame-ass musical in seven. I don't like musicals, okay? Sue me. People just don't start singing for no reason. If they did they'd get a slug in the kisser.

The Set Decoration Department was beyond the lines of studios in a building that also housed the costumes, sets when they were being stored and whatever the hell else they used to make movies. I had to turn left at the street of studios – the *Avenue of Stars* was what Centurion called it. I probably could have followed a quiet path I'd seen running down one side of the studios. I'd remember that for when I left. I wasn't doing anything illegal – at least not that I knew of – but all the same, best keep my visit quiet. It's just how it is in my business.

I passed a harried-looked broad pushing a rail of costumes as I entered the building. 'Set decoration?' I asked.

'Do I look like a directory enquiries?' she snapped back.

'No, you look like somebody who doesn't know where she's going herself.'

She was going to give me sass but instead she rammed the end of her rail into the doorframe. 'Now look what ya made me do.'

I pushed the rail to the side so it lined up with the door. 'There,' I told her, 'straight ahead. Now, Set Decoration?'

She nodded at a door. 'Straight ahead,' she parroted.

Why is everybody in the movies a wise ass?

I went through the doors she had indicated. The corridor was maybe twenty yards long. There were rooms to the right full of every damn thing you could imagine and a whole hell of a lot you couldn't. From there, Set Decoration was easy to find. The big sign over the door was a bit of a clue.

I went inside. It was a huge workspace full of benches, all covered with things that were to be heading for a movie set before long. I passed a bench covered with everything they'd need for a pirate flick. I guess they were trying to ape *The Sea Hawk*. Damn, that was a good picture, too. Errol Flynn and... not Olivia deHavilland for once. Some dame I'd never eyeballed before... Brenda Marshall, that was it. She was the Spanish Ambassador's niece in the movie. She sure didn't sound Spanish to me. Not unless Spain had moved to San Diego.

The bench of Egyptian items was all the way at the back. It was also unattended. A red haired woman in her thirties was on the next bench along. She was doing some damn thing to a pistol. Was she making it look dirty? It didn't matter.

'Can I help you, hon?' the red-head asked. She had a Bronx accent. Another New Yorker who crossed the country in search of fame – or at least sunshine after September.

I flashed my pearly whites. 'Yeah, I'm looking for Lisa Borden.'

Red was disappointed, then impressed. 'You Lisa's guy? She didn't say she had somebody new. About time too, if ya ask me. That last fella she dated was never good enough for her. She spent half her dates slapping his hands away if you get my drift.' She pointed the pistol at me. 'So none of that. She deserves better. But hey, so do I.'

I interrupted before she bored me to death. That would look real bad on my gravestone. 'Is she here?'

Red shook her head. 'I'm sorry, hon. She's out for the rest of the day. Getting some work done on a few things.'

I looked blank. That's not unusual, trust me.

'She didn't tell you?'

I shook my head.

Red carried on, 'I think she's getting some advice on... yeah, I think it's dirt.'

'Dirt?'

Red held up the pistol she was covering with fake cobwebs. 'The magic of the movies, hon. Sometimes you gotta have grime as well as shine.'

That was a line she'd used before. While she'd said it I'd

been casting an eye across Lisa Borden's bench. The bird statue wasn't there.

Damn it.

I'm not saying I'd have swiped it if the thing had been lying there... but if anybody thinks that, they won't get an argument from me.

'Will she be back today?' I asked.

Red shook her head. Her hair was set so solid it didn't move an inch. 'She said she'd be back in the morning.'

I had to push my luck. 'Did she say where she was going?'

'Oh, you got it bad, don't you, hon?' She sighed. 'Lucky Lisa. But not so lucky you. She didn't say. You could catch her at home.'

'I don't think so.'

Red's carefully plucked eyebrows raised. 'Don't tell me. Her dad don't like you.' She shook the helmet of hair again. 'Don't worry. He don't like anybody who dates his daughter.'

This was getting too complex. I was too deep in too many lies. Best to shut it down. 'Nothing like that,' I said. 'I'm working tonight.'

'Doctor?' Red asked hopefully. 'Every girl wants to date a doctor.'

'Detective,' I answered. 'Bad guys do bad things at night. It's inconvenient but it's a fact.'

'Cop, huh?'

I didn't put her right. I'd said I was a detective. That was true. It was pretty much the only honest thing I'd said since I got to the studio. In this job you learned how to stretch the truth. It wouldn't have surprised me if I was a better actor that the schmucks in the pictures.

'I suppose I could risk phoning her at home,' I said.

'Brave boy,' Red said, a grin breaking across her face. Her lips carried too much lipstick.

I shrugged. 'I would be if she gave me her number.'

She gave me a sympathetic look. 'Hate to break it to ya, hon. Maybe she just didn't want to see you again.'

I played up the charm. I can do charm when I have to. 'Neah.' I gave my cutest smile. 'Who could turn this down?'

'Not me,' Red shrugged. 'But I got ten years and thirty

pounds on Lisa.'

'Some of us go for those pounds.' Yeah, I was playing her. I should have felt like a heel.

I didn't.

Blame the job.

She played along with the flirting. 'If Lisa and her dad scare you off you know where I am.'

I looked disappointed. 'I'd hoped to see Lisa tonight.'

Red shrugged again. 'Well, I can't give you her number.'

'Aw…'

She looked at me, really giving me the once over. 'But if you're brave enough to risk her old man, I will mention that the boss – he works over there – has a list of numbers.' She indicated a guy who did too much eating and not enough exercising. 'But I never told ya nothin',' she added meaningfully.

I grinned. 'And I never heard nothin'.'

I liked Red. She was honest and open. She was a flirt and she didn't hide it. She wanted a good guy and she deserved one. In this town it was more likely she'd land a bum who'd treat her like dirt. He'd walk out in five years when the red had started coming from a bottle.

'But thanks,' I added.

'Thank me by taking my number as well, just in case.'

I just winked in reply.

I passed the bench Red had pointed at. A list of numbers was typed on a sheet of paper. I've got a good eye and a good memory. I didn't even have to slow down to get Lisa Borden's number stuck in my memory. I didn't look for Red's. I wasn't being a heel. Just the opposite. She deserved a good guy. That ain't me.

I heard a couple of European accents talking at one of the tables as I left. Hollywood was full of Europeans then. I guess it has been since the first white guys decided to take this place from the Indians. When I see what kind of mess the Europeans are making over there I wonder if this place would have been better off without them.

I turned and followed that quiet little path back to the parking lot. It wasn't particularly quiet either. I could hear the thump of feet and the loud music from one studio. Damn, I hate musicals.

There was gunfire as I passed the back of another. There were guns and screams from one of the other studios.

I drove out of the studio and wondered who the hell you talked to in a city like this about dirt. My job was to get *the dirt* on people but that wasn't what I was thinking about. It had to be historical dirt, right? So what did that mean? A museum? A university? A library? I wouldn't be at home in any of those places. The books I like come from newsstands and dime stores, not libraries.

I did some more thinking as I drove. If I waited till morning, Lisa Borden would talk to her buddy, Red. That would mean there would be questions when we met. She'd have a bad opinion of me straight off. My best bet was to contact Lisa that night. I still had my shield from the old days as a cop. Hanging onto it was a perk of doing the job all those years. It was also illegal but I didn't give a damn. It was useful to have.

I had written down Lisa Borden's number is my notebook. When I got back to the office I decided to take a chance and called it. An older woman answered. Just from her voice I could tell she was a church-going, god-fearing, salt-of-the-Earth woman – the type I avoided like a sober weekend. They made me feel guilty.

'Who is it?' Ma Borden asked.

'Detective Mitchell Stone,' I answered.

Her voice went up about five octaves. 'Detective? You're a cop? What's happened? What's wrong? Is it Lisa? Has something happened to Thomas?'

I didn't answer the question about being a cop directly. If I didn't answer, I couldn't lie, right? 'I'm looking for your daughter, Mrs Borden,' I said. 'She's not in trouble. I just think she might have accidentally witnessed something and I hope she might be able to help me.'

You could hear the woman's breathing go back to normal. She stopped panicking. 'Lisa's at work today,' she said. 'She'll be back around six thirty.'

'I've just been to the studio,' I told Ma Borden. 'Lisa's friend – the redhead – told me Lisa was out this afternoon but she didn't know where exactly. Or she couldn't remember.'

'Redhead? That's Meggie. Nice girl but a bit of a scatterbrain, if you ask me...'

'I was wondering if you knew where Lisa was this afternoon,' I interrupted. I never had time for gossips and I was too old to start. 'If I can talk to her this afternoon it'll all be over in no time.'

She *hmphed* at me. *Bitch*. If I'd still been a real cop I'd have arrested her for that "hmph". 'She's at the Carnegie Museum,' the old bag said, 'though I don't know what she sees in that job...'

I interrupted again. I was being an asshole and I didn't care. Not for five hundred bucks. 'Thanks. I'll catch her there,' I said and hung up.

She was probably still speaking. Whether she thought she was speaking to me or was tearing me a new one for hanging up, I didn't care. The Carnegie Museum was half an hour's drive from my office. With luck I'd have it all sorted by the end of the afternoon and within twenty four hours I'd be five hundred bucks better off.

The Carnegie is a swanky joint. It was built just after 1900 but it has that look of being old. Really old, like it's two hundred years older than it is.

It took a while to find Lisa Borden. I was told she was meeting with a guy in the Egyptian exhibit. I'd been told to look for a guy who looked like a professor. That would be Mr Argyle. They were right. He looked like a professor. A balding head with wild tufts of hair and a moustache that had escaped captivity long ago. I guessed he was maybe sixty but he could have been eighty. It wasn't a surprise he knew about history. He'd lived through most of it.

Lisa Borden had her back to me. She was staring at a tray of old artefacts still coated in dirt. She was making notes and taking pictures with some new type of camera.

I got my defunct badge ready so I could get the lie told. 'Miss Borden? Lisa Borden'

She turned and looked up at me. 'Yes?'

I've been in this town a long time. It's full of good looking dames. Lisa Borden hit me like a bucket of cold water. She was pretty. Damn, she was pretty. Cute with a mouth that always looked ready to smile... and smart eyes. The kind of eyes that knew what a guy was thinking and already had a comeback lined up for whatever line the dumb mook tried to throw her. Her blonde hair was thrown to the side giving her a hint of Veronica Lake but when she stood up she moved with the grace and ease of Ginger Rogers. She was tall, too. I liked them tall. At six-two I got no choice.

She was looking at me with those smart eyes. She had something of Olivia deHavilland or Paulette Goddard in those eyes. Something of them but plenty that was all her own.

Damn it. I just hadn't expected her to be so pretty. I am one shallow son-of-a-bitch. I kicked my ass into gear. 'Miss Borden, I'm Mitch Stone. I'm a private detective.'

Well, shit. I screwed that.

She looked intrigued and kinda amused. 'You are? Am I being investigated? Are you a shady ex-cop?'

I took out my badge. 'How did you guess?'

'You've got the look.'

'Is that an insult or a compliment?'

'Yeah.' Damn, she was a firecracker all right. 'So, what can I do for you, Mr Stone?'

Her question got my brain back on the rails. 'You bought a bird,' I said. 'An Egyptian bird.'

'That's right,' she agreed. 'It cost a buck and my boss still went nuts but I think it's worth every cent.'

It was worth a hell of a lot more to me. 'Thing is, it wasn't the shop's to sell,' I told her. 'The guy who hired me bought it, but it got stuck in with the shop's stock by mistake. They didn't own it. They shouldn't have sold it.'

'And you want it back?' I hated how disappointed she sounded.

Not enough to give up on my five hundred bucks. 'Afraid so.'

She screwed up her nose in disappointment.

'But the boss says have to reimburse you for the statue,' I lied. 'Would ten bucks be okay?'

She just looked at me, taking my measure. It wouldn't take long. I never had much character and none of it was good. 'Ten bucks will be fine,' she said finally. She winked. 'Let's keep the ten bucks between you and me, though. I can get a replacement falcon from a dozen shops for a quarter and use the rest to get some extra pieces for the set.'

I kinda liked that she wasn't putting the ten dollars in her pocket.

'Do you have it with you?' I asked.

She shook her head making that blonde hair shimmer. 'It's back at the studio. One of the guys is cleaning it for me overnight.'

That explained why it hadn't been on her desk.

'Could we get it tonight?' I asked.

She agreed. 'Sure. I'm pretty much done here. Say, you got a car?'

'Yeah.'

She glanced at her watch. 'Great. That means I might be on time.'

'You got a date tonight?' Why did I ask that? And why did I want to know the answer?

She just looked amused. 'You got something in mind? Fast mover, huh?'

I answered sass with sass. It's all I had. 'Do you always have a smart mouth answer for everything?'

'Better than having a dumb answer for everything,' she shot back. 'And no, I don't have a date. My folks like to eat at seven. Well, my Dad likes to eat at seven and that means everybody eats at seven.'

I'd been right. It was an old school kind of house. Dad ran the show. It was pretty clear that Miss Lisa Borden didn't much care for that though. I liked the rebel spirit.

'I'll drive you home after we pick up the bird,' I told her.

'Will you now?' She was teasing me now.

'Well, I'm offering to.'

She nodded, shimmering that hair. 'It's been a long day and you used to be a cop so I guess I can trust you. Probably.'

'Yeah, you can. Probably.'

Her eyebrows went up playfully. 'As far as I can throw you.'

Somehow I just didn't think I was in charge of the conversation anymore. 'The offer is there to drive you home, okay?'

She nodded. 'I'm taking you up on it.'

Half an hour later we were back at the studios. Miguel Rodriguez was still manning the gate. He looked shaken. Hell, he was gray.

'What is it, Miguel?' Lisa asked.

The security guard was damn surprised to see Lisa. Relieved, too. 'You're okay, Miss Borden.'

'Why wouldn't I be?'

'The shootings...' Miguel shook his head. That was pretty much when Lisa Borden and I both looked up and saw the cops running around and bodies being carried on stretchers towards ambulances.

I recognized the cop running the show. Bill Donohue. One of the good guys. Or at least one who wasn't bought and paid for. I parked and we went straight to Donohue.

His greeting was as friendly as I'd expected. 'What the Hell are you doing here, Stone?'

'Bringing the lady back to work,' I answered.

Donohue eyeballed Lisa and decided he didn't believe me. 'Right.'

'It's the truth,' Lisa said. 'What happened?'

'What's it to you?' Donohue snarled.

'I work here.'

'And I was here a couple of hours back,' I added. 'Maybe I can help.'

That interested Donohue. He saw a chance to get info on the cheap. 'Sure. What time were you here?'

I told him.

He sucked his lip, looked disappointed. 'You must have missed whoever did this by a few minutes.'

'What happened?' I asked.

Donohue lit a smoke. Didn't offer me one either. Cheap bum. 'A bunch of foreign accents showed up and shot up the people who design the stuff that goes on set.'

'Oh, my god.' Lisa Borden paled in front of my eyes. That had to be Set Decoration Department that had been shot up. Her workplace. Her friends.

I stayed professional. 'That's where I was. I was doing a bit of work. Private Eye work.'

Donohue snorted. I hated the look on the son-of-a-bitch's face. 'What else would you be doing? You ain't smart enough to be a lawyer and you ain't decent enough to be a priest.'

'And you ain't sharp enough to be a detective but that's how it is.' I shot back. That didn't do me any good. I needed to be reasonable. 'Look, I'll tell you what I can.'

Lisa Borden drifted away while I gave Donohue a brief version of the story. I left out the bits that would lead to difficult questions. I wasn't risking my five hundred bucks.

Lisa came back. Those beautiful eyes were full of tears. Her friends had been shot up. Had to be tough for the kid. She had blood on her blouse. She wouldn't go that close unless it was somebody...

Red.

She just looked at me.

'Meggie?' I asked. 'Red hair?'

Lisa nodded. 'They beat her. She might not live.'

She didn't need to say more. I got the picture.

They'd half killed Red.

She was a good woman. She had been working, doing her job.

They had beaten her half to death.

Bastards.

They were going to pay for that.

CHAPTER FOUR

Good things and bad things about visiting the past. Horrific torture garments masquerading as underwear has already been mentioned. Lack of wifi is also an utter bugger. As is the lack of mobile phones, Facebook, general internet, *Netflix* and everything else that makes us such a pampered bunch in the Twenty-First Century.

We had to make do with the wireless. The sponsorship of those old radio shows is either brilliantly awful or appallingly awful. I'm not sure which. Might be both, really. The shows weren't much better to be honest. The comedy was... well, without being totally immersed in the time, all of the pop-culture references sailed over my head. Helena laughed at some of them, though. But never forget she is very, very old. Some of the drama stuff was okay and you know what? I really like big band music. I knew some Glenn Miller stuff. I mean, everybody's seen *The Glenn Miller Story*, right? It's on every Christmas. But there were a whole load of other bands on the wireless. I really enjoyed the music. My credibility is dead. I don't care.

Before we all traipsed off to our beds we heard a news report saying there had been an incident at Centurion Studios but the police were staying tight-lipped. The news reporter said he hoped nobody had accidentally swapped live rounds for blanks. That was his big ho-ho at the end of the bulletin. *Insensitive prick!* He didn't know if anybody was hurt but there he was, making a cheap laugh out of it. Knob.

Helena and Ibrahim had taken the biggest of the bedrooms

on the left of the staircase. I told Erimem she could have the largest of the rooms off to the right.

'You are the star, after all.'

She nodded with that playful look in her eye she gets when she's relaxed and happy. 'I am also Pharaoh of all Egypt and a living god.'

'Yeah,' I agreed, 'that too.'

'Daughter of Light,' she added. 'That was a good title.'

'Whatever.'

'The Begetter of the Begotten.'

'You made that up.'

'No, I didn't,' she protested. 'Ooh, Guardian of the Gods, that's me.'

I nodded. 'Goodnight, Guardian.'

I gave her a hug and said another goodnight before settling into the best night's sleep I've had in ages.

Morning came, and with it our cleaning lady, a rather lovely Mexican lady named Rosa Carlita Mendez. She asked that we just call her Rosa. She was horrified that we insisted that she call us by our first names. It wasn't the done thing apparently, but she liked us anyway.

Helena took over the logistics of the house. She gave Rosa a roll of notes and told her to use the money for anything she needed for the house and then we abandoned the poor woman and went off so that Erimem could be discovered.

It's an odd thing knowing that you're going to be in a fight. We have been in many scraps since we started this time travel lark, but they've always crept up on us and just happened. Not this one. We knew where we were going, how many asses we were going to kick and whose neck we were going to save.

Waldo's Diner is probably the most stereotypical Americana diner in history. I doubt if there's ever been anything like it. It had the booths, the seats at the counter, the waitresses bustling about... We waited outside, quietly out of the way until we saw Carson Reed move from his seat inside. We'd recognised him from pictures we'd researched online before travelling to 1940. He was not as dapper in person as he was in the press shots. He was shorter than I expected, too.

'There,' Erimem said quietly. 'Three men are following him.'

She was right. Three musclebound gorillas were easing out of a booth to follow Carson Reed out of the diner. He turned and moved into a quiet alley, moving towards a car.

'Two more,' Erimem said.

'Five? He said there was only three in that interview.'

'He was wrong.'

With that Erimem was running. We didn't have a choice. We ran after her.

Reed saw that he was in trouble pretty quickly. He was surrounded by five guys, all of them mean-looking.

'Look,' he said,' if it's my wallet you want...'

One of the thugs had a face made of scars. 'We want it all,' he said. 'Your money, your watch, your car.' He smiled. His teeth were as ugly as his face. 'Your blood.'

His friends laughed. They were horrible laughs.

One of the stopped laughing as Erimem's knee slammed into his back. The force of the blow sent him face first into a wall. He fell unconscious, his face a mess of blood, broken nose and shattered teeth.

A second hood went for his knife. Too slow. She kicked him in the nuts. As he buckled forward she drove her knee up into his face. More blood. More teeth.

Two thugs down, two broken noses.

A third had also pulled a vicious looking knife. Erimem deflected it with a bin lid she had picked up. The thug pitched forward, losing his balance. He fell to his hands and knees. Before he could stand, Ibrahim kicked the knife from the hoodlum's hand. The thug pushed himself upright, straight into a punch from Ibrahim. He lurched towards me... lurched straight into a right cross. The best I've ever thrown. It shook me all the way up to my shoulder. Shook him all the way down to his boots. He was out cold on his feet when Ibrahim's left hook dropped him to the ground. The fourth member of the gang was already wearing the marks of picking a fight with Helena. She's got two and a half thousands years' worth of experience in kicking arse. She didn't need much to deal with this guy. *Whack! Whack! Head bounced off an iron railing.*

Four down and only Scarface left.

He stabbed at Erimem with his knife. She used the bin lid as a shield, deflecting the blow. He stabbed again. This time she deflected and swept the bin lid at Scarface's head. He grunted as she smashed the lid into his face. Remembering what we'd read, she swept up a knife dropped by one of the other goons.

He stabbed again. This time Erimem caught the blade against her own, deflected it and smashed the bin lid into his head. Another stab attempt, another parry, another smash in the face with a bin lid. He didn't learn. He tried again. This time she knocked the blade from his hand and kicked his knee out from under him. She slammed the bin lid into his face again, again, again. He slumped, unconscious.

Erimem spun. The first of the thugs she had attacked was staggering to his feet. She flipped the bin lid so she held it by the edge. She threw it like a big Frisbee. It hit him just below the knees and he landed hard on his face.

'*Captain America*,' Erimem smiled at me. 'I am glad you made me watch this movie.'

'Movie?' Carson Reed was looking at the five fallen hoods, and then his eyes settled on Erimem. 'Did you say you're in the movies?'

'Not exactly,' Erimem answered.

'But you want to be?' Reed asked.

'This is Hollywood,' Erimem repeated the words from Reed's magazine interview. 'Doesn't everybody want to be in movies?'

Reed looked again at the fallen hoods and then at my friend. 'Congratulations, kid. You just made the big time.'

CHAPTER FIVE

I drove Lisa Borden home. We had to give statements to the cops first. I'd worked hard to get as much information from them as I gave up. I held back on telling them about my employer. I wish I could say I did it because it helped solve the case. I did it because I didn't want to lose my five hundred bucks.

And I did it because I wanted to find the sons-of-bitches who half killed Red.

They killed the spark in Lisa Borden when they attacked her friend. She didn't talk on the way back to her parents' house. Maybe she was in shock. Maybe she had nothing to say. Maybe she linked me to the bastards who half-killed her friend.

The cops had no idea who had committed the murders or why.

I did.

Mr Gray had said there would be Europeans after the bird. When I had left the set decoration department there had been a bunch of Europeans coming in. I hadn't given them any thought. This is Hollywood. You hear every accent and see every kind of face in this town. Everybody comes to Hollywood. The place is full of Europeans who got out of the craziness over there. Half of the German movie industry upped sticks and got out of town when Hitler and his goons took power. Most of them came to Hollywood. Most of them are making damn good livings too like that guy Korngold who writes the great music for Errol Flynn's flicks. The ones that don't make it in the pictures still have skills they can use. A guy who ran a studio's cafeteria in Germany has a restaurant over here. Nothing German on sale there either. Maybe when Hitler's gone he'll cook German food again. Until then... everything but German.

Those Europeans in the set decoration department hadn't worked in any restaurant. They didn't work in the studio either.

But they had worked over Red. They had worked over three of the others who worked in the department. One of them was dead. It had looked deliberate to me. I had told Bill Donohue as much. He agreed.

'So,' he had asked me. 'Robbery gone wrong or something else?'

'You'll get that answer when one of those poor mugs can talk.' I nodded towards the ambulances. The victims of the attack were being loaded up. That wasn't much of an answer. I'd have to give Donohue more or I'd sound like I was being evasive. 'It's all guesswork till you have facts and you know as well as I do guesswork gets you nowhere. But if they was robbing somebody, why come here? A studio like this must have cash somewhere. Why come here? To this department?'

'Yeah,' Donohue nodded. 'It don't make sense and I get a gut-ache I don't like when it don't make sense.' Donohue was from Chicago, half-Irish half-Italian, all Catholic. Went to Confession every Friday and cried real tears while he told his priest about the skirt he was cheating on his wife with. Not a bad guy, just one who should never had got hitched. He had a decent cop's brain, though. 'This one just feels wrong, Stone.'

'I think you're right. I'm gonna keep my ear to the ground on this,' I told him. 'If I hear anything, I got your number.'

Donohue looked at Lisa Borden, sitting in a chair, trying not to see the chaos around her. 'So, what's the deal with you and the Borden dame? She a case or is she a different kind of work?'

Jesus H. Christ. Even in the middle of this, Donohue was looking for his next fling.

'A gentleman never answers that kind of question,' I told him, 'but she's got a big "hands off" sign in my handwriting. Got it?'

Donohue held his hands up in defeat. He was a cheating son-of-a-bitch but he knew you didn't play in a brother-in-blue's sandbox. He thought Lisa and me were together. Good, that kept him at arm's length. It also meant that the cops would put a bit extra into looking out for her. It's a perk of the job. Even after you quit, the boys look after you and yours.

I'd given some of what I knew to Donohue. He'd given back everything he knew and I picked up something real important. The sheet of paper with the phone numbers and addresses of the people working there was exactly where I saw it earlier. Those European bastards hadn't got it. That meant they didn't know where Lisa Borden lived. That was the only reason I was comfortable taking her home instead of to a safe house. Donohue agreed to pull in a couple of uniforms and have them watch the house all night. I made the pair of uniforms as soon as I drove up. They were exactly where I would have been, parked in an alley giving a good view of the front of the nice little house where Lisa lived with her folks. They were in the middle of four houses with another set of four sitting backyard to backyard behind them. Nobody was going to risk going in that way. Too many ways to be seen. No, these cops were in the right place. They were in a regular automobile, too. In daylight you could only see them if you were looking for them. At night they would just look like any other parked automobile.

I didn't tell Lisa the cops were there. She didn't need to be scared any worse than she was already. She had been quiet most of the way home but she made an effort to perk up when she saw her house.

'I've been terrible company,' she said. 'Especially after you were kind enough to drive me home.'

'You've had a shock. If you were telling jokes and doing cartwheels I'd be worried.'

'This skirt isn't designed for cartwheels.' She had tried to be funny. Her heart wasn't in it. 'Sorry. Look, you've been really kind driving me around today. Can I offer you coffee?'

'I shouldn't.' That was damn straight. I had work to do. On the other hand, I still had to find out *exactly* where Lisa had stashed the bird. I couldn't just sit there in the car and ask her. She'd tell me to go to Hell. I had to play it cool and schmooze her. 'Yeah, why not. I think we both deserve a coffee after today.'

The Borden house was nice. They were decent, respectable

people. I really didn't belong there.

They did care about Lisa, though. Got to give them that. Her mother almost keeled over when she saw the blood on Lisa's blouse. The parents interrogated me while Lisa changed her clothes.

Where had the blood come from?

Was Lisa hurt?

Was she in danger?

What was going on?

Why did a cop drive her home?

They didn't like that I was a private detective. Her mother thought I'd lied, misled her. She was right. I had.

Lisa saved me from being thrown out. She came back, dressed in a pink blouse and pale blue cardigan. 'Stone's working with the police,' she explained. 'He's helping them with the case.' She shrugged at me. 'I heard you talking to Donohue.'

'I knew him back when I was a cop. We worked together some.'

The news that I really had been a cop and still helped out calmed the parents some and they started listening instead of just asking questions. When I was a beat cop that was one of the first things I learned. After an incident people ask questions but don't listen to the answers. Asking the questions makes them feel they're doing something. They're just not ready for the answers until their heads have settled. It took a while for Lisa Borden's parents to settle. When they did, Lisa settled as well. Her parents frustrated her but Lisa loved them. They loved her back. It made me want to leave even more. Drunk parents had been my lot. When they were sober they didn't talk to each other. When they were drunk they just shouted. When they were really drunk, their fists talked. Both of them. I left when I was fourteen. I didn't know if they were alive or not. Didn't care either. They weren't part of my life.

This kind of warm family wasn't part of my life either.

I decided to go. Talking about the statue could wait until morning. 'I should leave you to have dinner.'

'You could join us,' Lisa offered. I'm not sure how well that played with Ma and Pa Borden.

You know something? I actually thought about it. 'That's a

nice offer but I have to work,' I said finally.

Lisa's eyebrow lifted. 'Is this work blonde or brunette?'

'It's bald and used to be a cop.'

Her attempt to be playful disappeared. 'You're chasing up something about the attack today.'

I didn't confirm that. 'Could be.' I didn't confirm it... not much. 'I should go,' I said. I nodded a goodbye to her parents and made for the door. I wasn't getting away so easy. Lisa followed me outside.

'I could come with you.'

I wasn't wearing that. 'And your dad could beat the living tar out of me if I took you anywhere dangerous.'

'We could tell him you're taking me to see a movie.' Yeah, Miss Nice-Gal suggested lying to her old Dad.

I shook my head. 'He'd kill me dead for sure if I suggested that.'

'Stone dead.'

I scowled. I'd heard enough cracks about my name over the years. 'Funny girl.'

She gave a little bow. 'I try.' She caught my arm. 'Stone, I appreciate everything you did today.'

There was too much in those eyes. Too many emotions. Hurt, anger, revenge, *something else*? That was a bad idea. Never get mixed up with dames from a case. That's a simple rule. I learned that early. I just never learned it about anybody who looked like Lisa Borden. I gave her my most reassuring smile. The one I first sergeant taught me. 'I'm just glad you're okay.'

She seemed to accept that she was benched for the night's investigation. 'Can you believe they want us back at the studio tomorrow? We'll have to double shift to cover for...'

Yeah, Red's attack sneaked up on her there.

'You'll have security watching out for you?' I asked.

She shrugged, little shoulders up and down miserably. 'They didn't say.'

'You will,' I said confidently. 'I'll talk to Donohue.'

She scrutinized me. 'You think we'll need it?'

'I think you needed it today when you didn't expect to.'

She grimaced. 'You're not encouraging, Stone.'

It was my turn to shrug. 'Sorry, I never learned that trick.

How will you get to the studio in the morning?'

'Same as usual. Bus.'

I didn't like that. Buses were too open. Anybody could get on beside her. She was my way to the other half of my five hundred bucks. That's what I kept telling myself. 'I'll pick you up at eight.'

Her head tilted. 'You're presuming a lot.'

'I'm presuming you'd rather ride in my car than on a bus.'

She conceded that. 'You might be right.'

'I'm a detective. It happens sometimes.'

'You should still be a cop.'

'How do you work that out?'

'Because you're a good guy. You like helping people.'

I resorted straight to wise-ass. 'You repeat that to anybody and I'll sue. That kinda talk could put me out of business.'

That hair shimmered as she shook her head. 'You don't fool me, Stone.'

I pushed her front door open. 'Go and eat with your folks.'

She stopped halfway into the house. 'Sure you won't join us?'

It was still tempting but I had to refuse. 'I'm not house trained. I'm not even allowed on furniture most places I go. Goodnight.' I turned to go. Her voice stopped me.

'Hey, Stone.'

'Yeah?'

'You didn't mention the statue once this afternoon.'

'Didn't I?'

'You know you didn't.'

'I guess my memory ain't what it used to be.'

'Neither is your grammar.' She looked at me. *Into* me. Like all the barriers of bluster and bull didn't exist. 'You put on this tough guy act. The talk is fake. You're as big an actor as anybody at the studio.'

I didn't have a good answer to that. 'Goodnight, Lisa Borden. See you in the morning.'

'Goodnight, Stone. And make it *seven* tomorrow morning,' she added. 'I've got an early start.'

Every guy has some girl in his past that tore his heart out and stomped on it just for giggles. If he's lucky he meets the woman who picks up that heart, dusts it down and starts it beating again. Guys in my job usually don't get that second chance. We just go through the first part of the deal over and over again. That's just how it is. Lisa Borden was the kind of girl who made me wish things were different. That *I* was different.

But I wasn't. A lion's got to be a lion, a scorpion's got to be a scorpion, a wolf's got to be a wolf. And I've got to be what I am.

Even if that meant ending up alone and alcoholic or dead.

Sounds overly dramatic?

Tell me how many old Seamuses you know. If the number is taller than none you're a damn liar.

I got in the car and drove away.

CHAPTER SIX

Okay...

I must stop sounding like I'm reading Sam Spade.
I must stop sounding like I'm reading Sam Spade.
I must stop sounding like I'm reading Sam Spade.

There's something in the air here. It's making me talk like I'm in an old movie.

Maybe it's because I've been to an old movie studio.

As soon as the cops had done their thing and taken statements from everyone, we had left the area. We'd had to get past a bunch of journalists and cameramen. Carson Reed had called them so he could publicise his new find.

Erimem.

He told the cops and then the journos how Erimem had fought off all five thugs on her own. I knew that was the story he'd tell. Somehow a journalist was going to mess that up and make it just three scumbags. It still pissed me off that the rest of us were overlooked. We had kicked ass, too. Then we'd kicked balls.

There I go again.

This sounding like I'm Humphrey Bogart stuff... It's an illness, I tells ya, Mugsy.

Reed didn't mess about. As soon as the paparazzos (were they called paparazzi in 1940 or were they still a more respectable name?) had the pics they wanted – which they got without Erimem actually chinning any of them – we were whisked off to the studio.

I always expected a movie studio to be busy. I didn't expect it to be swarming with cops. Dozens of them.

The stressed-looking guy at the security gate explained. 'Somebody went nutso in the set decorators' place. Put three of them in the hospital, one in the morgue.'

'Jesus. Who died? Will be others be okay?' Reed actually sounded genuinely concerned. 'Who the hell would do that?'

'Nobody that works here. They went past us claiming to be extras. They had stolen passes.' The security guard sounded like he knew he was going to carry the blame for this. I suppose not much has changed. He was Latino. When there's blame to be handed out, look for the minority.

We were stopped twice by cops wanting to know who we were before we reached an office block. Reed's office was on the second floor. Well, I call it an office. It was more like a store room for scripts. They were on the desk, on the table, on the spare chairs. What little wasn't covered in scripts was covered in drawings of costumes, sets and props. The place was full of paper. Health and Safety wouldn't be invented for another forty years but they were screaming in protest anyway when Reed lit a smoke.

'First thing is we get you on a contract,' Reed said. He called the legal department. Less than five minutes later Erimem was signing a contract.

And so was I.

How did *that* happen?

Well, it was Helena's fault. She mentioned that she and Ibrahim were from an international talent agency based in London. They had brought a couple of clients here to LA to see if there was interest in us. Erimem and Andrea Smith, was how she introduced us, before pointing out that we were sisters.

You could see Reed's brain implode. *Sisters?* Erimem's North African and I'm pasty-white British.

'We have different mothers,' Erimem said.

Well, that was honest. We did have different mothers. But we had different fathers, too. And different brothers – because we're not bloody related. Having said that, you know, in London 2018 it wouldn't be a big deal for us to be sisters. Nobody would bat an eyelid. In 1940 Los Angeles it would definitely be a thing.

That didn't stop Reed from looking at me – I mean actually noticing me - for the first time. You could hear his mind whirring. He was working out how to use the sisters angle in a movie. It was always about the angle. If us being sisters was a thing it was a thing he was going to use. He could hear cash registers ringing.

Erimem got a contract on what sounded like pretty good money from what I could remember of salaries for the time here. Mine was fairly decent too but I was a "developmental" contract. That meant they could pay me less till they worked out their sisters angle. Even though I had no intention of ever being on screen I was still miffed that I got a crappier contract. Does that make me shallow? We all thought so when we were laughing about it later.

As soon as the contracts were signed Reed dragged us down to the costume department. While Erimem got measured, Reed looked me over and asked if I could sing.

'Nope,' I answered. 'Not a note.'

That didn't bother him. 'We'll dub you. Gloria's got a great set of lungs but a face for radio, if you get my drift.'

I got his drift. He was lucky I didn't drift my fist into his face.

I'm not the girliest of girls. Nothing to do with me being gay. Stereotype much? Shame on anybody who thought it was. I just prefer jeans and a t-shirt to a fancy dress but I will say that the evening gown the dresser shoe-horned me into was pretty spectacular. Teal green, I'd say. In black and white it would look a sort of ivory-white, apparently.

She nodded in the general direction of my chest. 'It'll need let out some if we want to stay decent.'

'As long as it doesn't let *them* out, I'm fine with it.'

She laughed. 'Don't worry, hon, you're not the only one with this problem. These dresses could keep a herd of buffalo in check.'

They did a quick make-up test then then plonked a black wig on my head for a fitting. It covered half of my face.

Shit.

I actually was *in* the film. In the shady background of the nightclub scene there was a torch singer in a slinky dress crooning *Begin the Beguine* in front of a big band. *That was me!*

Damn, I'd had a pervy moment thinking she looked really fit. Does it count as leching when you accidentally fancy yourself?

And god, my boobs do look big on screen!

So, I was going to be in a movie. Erimem came out of her side room. She was also wearing a wig. Hers was old Egyptian in style. So was her dress. Well, they were *sort of* Egyptian. We'll call them *Hollywood Egyptian*.

Erimem tugged at her wig. 'This is completely wrong.' The dress got her grouching next. 'So is this. The colour is wrong and the detail is not subtle enough.'

Reed bustled in without bothering to knock. If he'd done that fine minutes earlier he'd have worn his contracts as suppositories.

'It's for the camera,' he said. 'It can't pick up fine detail, and unless you're some kind of expert...'

'She is.' Helena had followed Reed in. Ibrahim was a gentleman and stayed outside until Helena yanked him inside the room. 'They're decent.'

'Just barely,' Reed said, looking at the front of my dress. 'Fix those before the censor fixes us.'

He shoved a script into Erimem's hand. 'Look, I know you're not experienced so we'll cut the dialogue short but I need to know you can deliver a line.'

'Shouldn't you have found that out before you gave me a contract?' Erimem asked reasonably.

He didn't give a damn. 'Listen, Toots, I've been looking for my Warrior Queen of the Nile for ten weeks. I tried to get a couple of the gals who played villains in MGM's Tarzan flicks but they're out of our price range. RKO won't release Grace Gifford... hell, I even looked at theatre actresses and everybody knows they're a pain in the ass.' He snorted. 'Think they're too good for the movies. Nobody came close. You're doing the movie even if I have to cut all the dialogue.'

'Give her the script and see what you think,' suggested Helena.

Erimem plucked the script from Reed's hand and flipped through it.

Reed didn't look comfortable at the way the situation was being taken out of his hands. Probably because it was a bunch of us dames doing it. 'Okay,' he said slowly. 'How about...'

Erimem cut across him. 'My name is Ann-Ankh-Aten,' he said, exactly as we'd seen her deliver it when we watched the film. 'If you insult me again, remember this. I have crossed the boundaries of time to halt an ancient evil. A puny thing like you will not even slow me.' She stared at Reed. I mean she gave him the full scary-bitch stare. The one I've seen her wear when she's really going into battle and she knows people are going to die. *That* stare.

Reed's mouth sounded dry. 'I'm not cutting a word,' he said quietly. 'Keep the script, get learning it. Your first few scenes are filmed tomorrow so you don't need to know any lines. And you,' he said, turning to me. 'Yeah, I think you're going to be in here getting that fitted all day tomorrow. You're on set the day after for a nightclub scene.'

'Okay,' I said.

And that was that. We were on target with the mission. We'd met and saved Carson Reed. Erimem was going to be a movie star. I needed to find out if I had an IMDB page.

It was an average day for us really.

CHAPTER SEVEN

I drove back to the office and called a few old buddies from the force. The attack at Centurion was the talk at the houses across the city. Nobody knew too much. Donohue had landed a case to make a career. *Or kill it.* I got as much info as I could. That wasn't much. Turns out I knew more than most of the cops. I sashayed the conversation to other things. The sort of Seamus stuff they all thought they were too good for. I asked a few dummy questions to throw them off the scent. Had they heard anything about a New York hood fresh in the city? Did the name Frankie Mulcahy mean anything? Who was best to talk to these days if I wanted to find out about somebody new to the city?

I knew they would go searching for Frankie Mulcahy. Good luck to them. The only man by that name I knew was a priest. One of his altar boys had been dipping his hand in church funds. I caught the little ass-hole. Mulcahy let him go and gave him money. That was four years ago. The thief has spent the last three months pounding a beat here in LA wearing blue. The priest saw something I didn't. He turned a thief into a cop. How long would it take the job to turn him back again?

As well as my fun with Mulcahy, my calls gave me a name. *The Dutchman.*

Nobody knew exactly what the Dutchman's real name was. Nobody knew if he was really Dutch either. He had the accent but this is Hollywood. Lots of people have accents here. Sometimes more than one.

The Dutchman had the *Amsterdam*, a club in a part of town

that was too downmarket to be swish but it had a good enough reputation to bring in a better crowd. He also got the best music acts in his place. Word was he even got Tommy Dorsey's kid singer Sinatra in there for a few nights. Without Dorsey. That meant the Dutchman was connected.

There's an etiquette to follow when you go into a man's club looking for information. If he's small potatoes you can crash in, shake him up and get what you need. The Dutchman was nobody's small potatoes. He had to be treated with respect.

I bought a double Scotch at the bar. I didn't touch it but ordered another. The bartender knew what was coming. He had sharp eyes. They looked to the gorillas around the room, making sure they were around if I caused trouble.

I wasn't there for trouble.

'My name's Stone,' I said. 'Would you ask the Dutchman if it would be possible for me to have a few minutes of his time, please?'

The bartender's eyebrow lifted. I guessed it did that when he was thinking. And I guessed the only way he could count to eleven was to put both hands in his pockets and count his fingers.

'And two more double Scotches,' I added.

He poured again and gave the smallest nod to a human wardrobe standing by an inner door.

The wardrobe lumbered across. 'Come with me.' His voice was so deep it must have registered on the Richter Scale.

I followed the wardrobe across to the door. He knocked and waited for an answer.

'Come.'

Wardrobe opened the door and gave a slight movement with his head, sending me inside.

The Dutchman liked his comforts. He sat behind a desk the size of a decent city block. Leather couches were against expensively papered walls. The artwork was classy, the carpet was expensive and the broads were gorgeous. Bought and paid for, too, I guessed.

The Dutchman was about fifty, lean, tanned and under that suit he looked muscular. His hair was still thick and his own. The color wasn't. That told me he was vain enough to dye it.

I waited for him to speak first. This was the Dutchman's turf.

It wouldn't be respectful if I spoke first.

'Welcome to my club,' he said. Yeah, he really did have an accent but his voice was cool and measured. It worried me that it was quite friendly. 'How can I help you, Mr...?'

'Stone,' I said. 'Mitchell Stone. Thank you for seeing me.'

'Mitchell Stone?' the Dutchman's lips pursed. 'There used to be a police detective named Mitchell Stone, I believe.'

My cop buddies hadn't been joking. The Dutchman did know everybody.

'I used to be a cop,' I nodded. 'Now I'm just a private eye.'

That didn't impress him much. 'What are you investigating, Mr Stone? A cheating wife? A lost cat?'

I didn't change my tone. Kept it respectful. 'Four people were attacked at Centurion Studios today. Three are in hospital, one went straight to the morgue.' That had caught his interest. 'One of the three in the hospital is a woman. A good woman.'

'*Your* woman?'

I shook my head. 'Her friend is... her friend is a friend of mine.'

'Ah,' the Dutchman nodded. 'A *friend*.' He was reading something into it. Good. Let him think this was personal, not business. 'You have my sympathy, Mr Stone,' he said and I think he meant it, 'but how can I help.'

'You read the comings and goings in this city better than anyone,' I said. 'Nobody new comes in to LA without you knowing.'

'So I hear.'

'I think this attack was carried out by four Europeans. Skinny is they had German accents.' I had guessed at the accents from my own memory and what I'd picked up from everyone I spoke to.

The Dutchman licked his lips slowly and nodded. 'Four German gentleman arrived by seaplane a few days ago. They have money and they have connections. They were able to disappear completely within minutes of coming ashore.'

'Well, that's not suspicious.'

'Everything from Germany is suspicious,' the Dutchman said. He didn't hide his anger. 'They invaded my country, enslaved my people, killed thousands of us. Four of them arriving and going to ground is very suspicious indeed.' He poured himself a drink. 'What will you do if you find these men, Mr Stone?'

I wasn't owning up to anything. Especially in advance. 'That depends how nicely they answer my questions.'

'If you find their answers unpleasant?'

'My Smith and Wesson can be pretty unpleasant, too.'

The Dutchman liked that. 'I have been wondering about these four men,' he said. 'When they arrived and disappeared I started making enquiries.'

'Can I ask if you found anything?' I stayed all respectful.

The Dutchman flicked a hand and the two broads slinked through an inner door. He waited until the door closed before he spoke again. 'They have visited a number of antique shops,' he said, 'many of them dealing in esoteric and indeed, the occult.'

'Really?'

The Dutchman sneered. 'Their idiotic little Fuhrer is supposed to be obsessed with the occult.'

'I heard the crazy son-of-a-bitch was obsessed with Jews, too,' I answered.

That hit a nerve. He flinched just slightly. The Dutchman was either Jewish himself or he was worried about people who were. 'That, too,' he said. He rubbed his chin and scrutinized me for a long minute. 'I am going to help you, Mr Stone,' he said. 'I have a list of shops they visited. It may not be complete but it as much as I have for now.' He lifted another sheet of paper. 'On this sheet is the license plate of an automobile seen near several of these shops. It is a rather large car but I do not yet have an address for the owner of the vehicle.'

'I can ask the uniforms who patrol the areas around the shops,' I answered. 'They tend to notice unusual cars.'

The Dutchman nodded once and handed the papers across. 'Here, Mr Stone.'

This had gone well but there was still the reckoning. 'I know nothing in the world is free,' I said. 'Would it be rude if I asked what the check comes to for this?'

'You came to me with respect,' the Dutchman said. 'You have a reputation for a clever mouth but you kept it under control. You bought drinks you didn't consume. All of that would stand you in good stead, but you are hunting Germans.' His face went cold and hard. 'I despise the Nazis, Mr Stone. I hate them with every fiber of my being. I hate what they have done to my country and my people... my family... and now they have brought their vile behavior here. For that reason there is no charge for this information but I have one request.'

The hairs on my neck stood up. This could be very bad. 'Please tell me,' I said, still all respectful.

'When it's done, when they are dead, come and tell me.' The Dutchman tapped a bottle of good Scotch. The real thing, shipped across from Scotland. 'When you tell me that, you and I will have a large drink on the house.'

My plan wasn't to just hunt down and kill these Germans but I wasn't going to disappoint the Dutchman. 'I always liked good Scotch,' I said.

That was enough for him. 'Then I look forward to our next meeting eagerly, Mr Stone.' He nodded and pressed a button on his desk. My audience with the king was done.

'Thank you,' I said. Two doors were opening. The broads came in through one. The Wardrobe stood in the other. Too bad I got the wardrobe. I thanked the Dutchman again and left. The Wardrobe closed the door behind me and led me to the exit.

'I should pay my bar tab,' I said.

I saw the bartender pouring the Scotch back into the bottle.

'On the house,' the Wardrobe rumbled.

That was it. A minute later I was back in my car, driving away. I wouldn't get much more done that night. It was late and even hoods needed their sleep.

I thought about sleeping in my office so I could get an early start. It wouldn't be the first time I'd done it.

No.

I was picking up Lisa Borden in the morning. I should look at least human for that. I drove home and made a few phone calls to desk sergeants I knew.

After a long day I fell into the deepest and soberest sleep I'd had in months.

CHAPTER EIGHT

None of us had really been prepared for the whirlwind of the day. We had known things would move quickly. They weren't just quick. They were sudden.

Save the director.

Go to the studio.

Get Erimem hired.

Accidentally get me hired as well. (Thanks, Helena Big-Mouth!)

Costume fitting.

Wigs and make up testing.

Last and not least though it probably should have been higher up the list, Erimem did her screen test.

Erimem had seen the movie so she knew exactly how to pitch the performance to exactly what we already knew Reed wanted but I was still surprised by how well she played it. I shouldn't have been. She was Pharaoh of all Egypt. She had to deal with the politicians of her time. Actors pretend for a living and so do politicians. Actors pretend to be other people. Politicians pretend to care about people. Maybe the two jobs aren't a million miles apart.

Back at the house we ate a cold supper. Cold but delicious. Rosa had left it out for us. She deserved a pay-rise for that. We ignored the booze. It had been a long day and we had a lot to do the following day, too. I think Ibrahim and Helena had something to do as well. I don't eavesdrop but sometimes you can't help hearing occasional words. Time travelling wasn't going to put these two off their baby-making schedule. Who knew you could schedule that kind of thing? Anyway, it's none of my business. If they're happy, that's all that matters. They'll be great parents.

They're crap agents, though. I don't even get my own dressing room.

Just as well I'm not a real actress. I'd be a real diva.

We rocked up to the studio on time the next morning at half past seven. We'd had a good breakfast and we were ready to get on with finding that statue.

I wasn't needed on set that day. Erimem was. She was being introduced to the rest of the cast. There were two heroes. One was what passed for a leading man. John Buttler. I don't want to be mean or body-shame here, but let's say Johnny's not The Rock. If he ever went to the gym it was only to use their canteen. He wasn't fat – just ordinary. He looked like a regular guy. Odd I hadn't seen him look like that in the film. Then again, I hadn't noticed that he was wearing a rug either. The studio's hair people were better at hiding the fact that he was wearing a wig than whoever sent this guy out this morning.

The leading lady – according to the script her purpose was to scream, faint and be rescued at fairly regular intervals – was rather unfortunately named. In 1940 Goldie Raines sounded like a movie star – even if the name was as fake as the blonde in her hair. In 2018, Goldie Raines would be the kind of porn star name you really didn't want a drunken pub game to give you. First pet's name? Goldie. First Street you lived on? Raines Avenue. *Ta-da - Goldie Raines*. Hang on, though. That name wasn't on the movie's credits when we watched it in 2018. At some point somebody decided to switch from her dodgy porn-star name to her real name, Clementine Reed. That was a relief. She didn't have reason to worry any of it anyway. In 1942 she'd marry some industrialist, give up acting and spend her life being much happier and more productive working for a children's charity she'd set up.

Peter Arthur, our second lead, wouldn't be so lucky. He was young, sandy-haired, handsome and with the potential to be a huge star. He would volunteer for the US army the day after Pearl Harbour. It's hard putting on a face and making small talk with someone you know is going to die on a beach in the Philippines in a few years.

I put my smile on and played nice.

I think I might be a better actress than I thought.

While my *sister*, Erimem, and I met the big names, Helena and Ibrahim went and did some backstage snooping. I'm not sure Ibrahim's really got snooping in his genes but in her millennia, Helena has picked up skills. She talks to people. They open up to her. Most people like her. She's loved-up so she's not threatening to the women. She's sympathetic and funny. Guys? Shallow ones like the view. Smarter ones appreciate the brain. They're all wasting their time. She's been in love with Ibrahim for over a hundred years. She does get people to talk, though.

'Hey, Toots,' she said. Her accent was as fake as our lead actor's hair. 'What's a doll like you doin' in a crummy joint like this?'

'You been drinking?'

She grimaced. 'I wish.' She was back to her own accent. Thankfully. 'How's the fitting gone?'

'Pretty well. I only had to threaten to kill one pair of wandering hands. How's your morning gone?'

'Snoopily,' Ibrahim answered.

Helena batted his arm. 'That's not a word.' She turned back to me. 'We've been digging. Finding out what we can.'

'And?'

'Not much.'

I scowled. 'That's not a great answer.'

'We sort of know where the statue is,' Helena offered.

Her tone hadn't convinced me it was all good news. 'Why do I feel there's a big but coming?'

She gave a wry smile. 'Comes to us all in the end.'

'*Boom-tish*. Get the pretty lady a coconut.'

She gave in and 'fessed up. 'You're right. The "but" is that the set decoration department is closed up tighter than a duck's arse.'

'Anybody getting in there?' I asked. I wasn't hopeful.

'Only the people who work there and the police.'

'Cops,' I corrected.

'Cops. Yes, the cops. You know, I've never had the urge to call them the rozzers before but now that I can't, I really want to.'

I totally got that. Time travel does strange things to your vocabulary. 'Ya big palooka.'

She grinned. You know, she really should have been in front of the camera. 'Is there a female version of palooka? Palookette?'

A thought came to me. 'Hey, there's no chance we'll run into you here, is there? You were around in 1940.'

She shook her head. 'No chance. I'm busy doing my bit for King and country back in Blighty. Casualties are arriving back in England by now. I'm pretty busy at a military hospital.'

'And multi-tasking as an agent,' Ibrahim said. 'I married a talented woman.'

'Damn right you did,' She agreed. 'It wasn't a write-off of a morning, though,' she told me. 'We found out who we need to talk to about the statue.'

'Who?'

'Lisa Borden.'

The name meant nothing to me. 'And she is?'

'Surrounded by rozzers at the moment,' she said.

'Cops, dear,' Ibrahim corrected.

Helena nodded. 'Them, too.'

'So how do we have a little chat with her?' I asked.

Helena looked unsure. 'And how do we make that chat look like we're not just trying to pinch the statue?'

'That is easy,' Erimem's voice came from the doorway.

There she was, all dolled up and looking like... well like an Egyptian princess, I suppose. Just for a change.

'How did the morning go?' Helena asked.

Erimem looked around to make sure we were alone before answering. 'This acting is very easy. I just say the words exactly as I remember seeing them on TV and Carson is really happy. He is calling me "a one take wonder". I'm not sure what that is. Is it a good thing?'

I reassured her. 'It's great. It means you're reliable.'

She looked pleased. 'Then it is good.'

'So what are you doing here?' Ibrahim asked. 'Saved the world already?'

'No,' she answered. 'It is lunchtime.'

I'd completely lost track of the morning. 'Lunchtime?'

'And we are going to the canteen.' Erimem made it sound like the Ritz.

If it was swanky I wasn't sure we'd all be welcome with the big names. 'We are? All of us?'

She nodded. 'Yes. Everybody goes there Technicians, actors, everybody eats together.'

Ibrahim saw where she was heading. 'Including the set decorators?'

The wig swished as Erimem nodded. 'Yes. I asked.'

'Aren't you a clever clogs?' Helena said appreciatively.

Erimem beamed. 'I think so.'

'So where's the canteen?' Ibrahim asked.

The smile disappeared. 'Oh. I didn't ask that.'

We found the canteen easily enough. The detective work was tough. We asked a cameraman and he took us there.

I have worked at the Uni café for a few years now. I have been run off my feet by hordes of the hungover, the stoned, the still asleep, the desperate for food to fuel the next shag... I have seen my café busy.

The Centurion canteen put my café to shame. Everybody from all eight films that were shooting on the lot was there. So were the office workers. Everybody ate together. Secretaries, technicians and actors mixed with cameramen, designers and the kids in their first ever jobs working as runners. It did my lefty heart good to see everybody queueing and eating in the same place. Actors didn't get to jump the queue – or cut the line as they say here.

The other good thing was that we were able to get pointed at Lisa Borden pretty quickly. She was sitting at an out of the way table. A cop mountain sat next to her. He wasn't in uniform but he had the look. The bulge under his arm said he had the pistol as well.

'Mind if we sit here?' Helena asked.

Muscles looked unsure about that. 'Do you know them?'

Lisa Borden shook her head. 'No.'

'We're the new kids on the block,' Helena said.

'European.' Muscles sounded... what? Angry? Scared? Aggressive? All of the above and a dozen more?

Helena answered. 'Some of us.'

'Ibrahim and I are Egyptian,' Erimam said.

Helena added. 'But we all live in London.'

Muscle-Mountain looked at us impassively. He was still weighing us up. 'So what brings you here?'

It was the blonde woman, Lisa Borden, who answered. 'I'd say the costumes and make-up are a giveaway, Stone.'

He looked at Erimem and me in our dolled-up state. 'You're in the movies?'

'We're in *your* movie,' Erimem said to Lisa.

Things seemed to fall into place for the blonde. That wasn't a crack, by the way. This was obviously no dumb blonde cliche. Not many are. There are dumb brunettes and dumb redheads too. Of both genders. 'Are you the girl who beat up the thugs?' Lisa asked.

'We all did that,' I answered. Yeah, it still rankled.

'I hear there were eight,' the Muscle-Mountain Lisa had called Stone said. 'Or was it ten?' He didn't believe a word of it.

'Just five,' Erimem answered.

'And you beat them all?'

One delicate eyebrow lifted. That's a sign Erimem's reacting to confrontation. 'You look surprised.'

Stone didn't try to hide his disbelief. 'Just wondering how a slip of a chick like you could take down five strong thugs on your lonesome.'

'I am *very* well trained,' Erimem said calmly. Too calmly for it to end well.

Stone gave a little laugh. 'Yeah. I'm sure you are.'

Bad move, pal.

'You doubt me,' Erimem said. She was colder than a bank manager's heart.

He didn't even try not to be condescending. 'No, but five

guys beaten by one dame? It don't seem likely.'

I felt Helena and Ibrahim wince at my side. He was talking himself into an ass-whipping.

'Attack me,' Erimem said mildly.

Stone looked blank. 'What?'

'You heard. The instruction was simple enough. Attack me.'

His arms went wide. 'Hey, I don't attack dames, okay?'

'Are you a coward as well as a braggart?' Erimem snapped. 'Listen...'

Erimem cut him off. She spoke to Lisa. 'You should have a better companion than this jackal. He does not have the courage to protect a woman.'

That riled Muscles. 'Listen, lady...'

He made his move, leaning forward. *Bad idea.* Erimem caught his tie and yanked hard. He lurched forward. Her hand moved so fast none of us caught it. She had scooped up a fork and held it a centimetre from the cop's eye.

'If you insult me again I will pluck out your eyes and feed them to my dogs.'

The cop sat back, looking stunned.

Lisa Borden caught his hand. 'Are you all right, Stone?'

He nodded slowly. 'Feeling kinda stupid.'

Erimem dropped the fork to the table. 'I have no interest in harming you. I came to congratulate Lisa Borden on her work on the set.'

Stone blushed. 'Oh. Now I feel *really* stupid.'

'Don't worry,' Helena said brightly. 'She wouldn't have fed your eye to the dog.'

'I don't have a dog,' Erimem admitted.

'See?' Helena was obviously hoping to get us back on track.

Stone eyed Erimem for a moment. 'You know how to defend yourself.'

'I was well trained.'

'She was a soldier,' Ibrahim explained. 'A very good one.'

Stone nodded slowly. 'That explains a lot.'

Lisa Borden was clearly keen to move on as well. 'Can I guess you're going to be the Warrior Queen of the Nile?'

Erimem nodded agreement. 'You can.'

'I guess you'll be doing your own stunts,' Stone said.

I fielded that one. 'She will. I won't be doing my own singing though.'

'That is a *very* good thing,' Erimem said.

'Cheeky mare!'

Helena shook her head in at us. 'Ignore them. They're only happy when they're bickering.'

Stone had managed to find his impassive mask again. 'That a fact?'

Lisa Borden invited us to sit. Stone didn't seem so keen on the idea, but he didn't argue. There was no doubt he was her guard-dog, though.

Helena started the schmooze. 'We heard about what happened yesterday.'

Lisa winced. 'I think everyone in the business has.'

'I'm glad you weren't hurt.' No doubting Helena was genuine there. 'Can I ask...'

'Where I was?' Lisa interrupted. 'Doing research.'

There were questions to follow that up, but we needed to build trust first so Helena let it go for now. 'I'm glad you're safe anyway.'

Ibrahim picked up the questioning. 'Does anyone know what they wanted? Money?'

Helena frowned. 'You don't have anything really valuable on the sets do you?'

'Such as?' Lisa asked.

'Jewellery? Historical pieces.'

Lisa was wary. 'Why do you ask?'

'Well, we're thinking of stealing them,' I answered with a smile.

Helena scowled at me. 'Or we might be worried that whoever did this might come back.'

Lisa looked satisfied. Stone... not so much. 'Right.'

Helena looked at us all then ploughed on. 'And we might be concerned that they stole something they really shouldn't get their hands on.'

'Such as?' Stone looked smug. He had known there was something hinky about us.

Lisa chose to answer. 'I think we all know what she's talking about.'

'Lisa, don't,' Stone warned but it was too late.

Erimem leaned forward in her seat. 'You know where the Falcon is.'

Lisa thought for a second. 'Yes.'

'Is it safe?' Erimem asked.

'Yes.'

'And you can't have it,' Stone said.

Erimem looked at him with interest. 'Why?'

'Because I've been hired to get it.'

'Really? By whom?' Erimem asked.

Stone shook his head. 'That's between me and my client.'

'The Falcon must not fall into the wrong hands,' Erimem said. She was quiet but firm.

Stone wasn't impressed. 'And where are the right hands?'

Erimem raised her palms. 'Here.'

Lisa nodded at Stone. 'It's owned by his boss.'

Ibrahim wasn't impressed. He had left the chat to us but he spoke up now. 'Really? Something stolen from an Egyptian tomb is never going to morally be the property of the buyer.

'And you're here to take it back to Egypt?' Stone asked.

Ibrahim shook his head. 'Not as such.'

'We will put it somewhere safe,' Erimem added.

Stone sat back. It was a confrontational pose. No, he didn't trust us. 'I don't get German accents from you. Any of you sprechen sie Deutsche?'

Ibrahim shook his head. 'The only German I know comes from *Allo Allo*.'

'A radio comedy,' Helena explained. 'Why do you ask about German accents?'

Erimem sat closer, eyes narrowing with interest. 'These Germans must be after the Falcon.'

I felt the connections click into place. 'You mentioned the Falcon was supposed to have magic... mystic powers? What kind of powers?'

Erimem's mouth quirked thoughtfully as she remembered. 'To raise the dead from eternal slumber and torment their souls until they fight like demons...'

I tapped the table in triumph. 'If Hitler's really obsessed with the occult, then this is his kind of thing.'

Stone began, 'I need...'

Erimem talked through him. She had a point of reference. *'Raiders of the Lost Ark?* Face melting.'

'Yes! That kind of thing.' Whatever you need there's always a movie reference to explain it.

Helena joined in. 'Raising the dead? He wants to go the full George Romero? Army of the Living Dead?'

Erimem nodded. 'Yes. He must not get the Falcon.'

'He ain't getting the Falcon,' Stone said firmly. 'It belongs to my boss.'

'Does it?' Lisa asked.

'You know it does.'

'Think about it, Stone,' Lisa said reasonably. 'I don't buy any cockamamie ghost legend about it but if it's been stolen from a tomb...'

'... then who cares?' Stone interrupted. 'The stiffs in those tombs are dust.'

'The dead in those tombs were people with families who loved them and who mourned their loss.' Erimem's voice dropped the room's temperature by twenty degrees. She was cold with rage at the way he dismissed the fate of her family. 'The passage of time does not change that they were loved and that their rest has been desecrated for profit.'

Stone wanted to argue. He looked to Lisa for support. She looked at him with so much disappointment I almost felt sorry for him. Only almost.

'Maybe profit is how we deal with this,' Helena said thoughtfully.

Erimem nodded. She saw where Helena was going with this.

'Miss Borden – Lisa – am I right in saying you agreed to return this statue to Mr... Stone, is it?'

Stone nodded. 'That's me.'

'And yes, I did,' Lisa agreed.

Helena continued, 'And you, Mr Stone, are being paid to return the statue to someone who claims to own it?'

'Yeah.'

'Perhaps we can offer a financial inducement to you to pass it to us instead?'

'A financial inducement?' Lisa repeated. 'That sounds like a bribe.'

Stone agreed. 'It definitely is a bribe.'

Helena stayed business-like. 'I'd have said we were buying your release from your current contract.' She waited for an argument. None came. 'How much are you being paid for this job?'

Stone took a moment to answer. He looked at Lisa uncomfortably before going on. 'Five hundred,' he said. 'Five hundred up front. The same on delivery.'

Lisa's jaw dropped. 'A thousand dollars?'

'Well, it ain't a thousand jelly beans,' he answered.

Helena nodded. 'And if we offer you *two* thousand?'

This time it was Stone's jaw that dropped. 'Two grand?'

CHAPTER NINE

Two grand.

I never had the chance of that kind of dough.

Two grand.

Two thousand bucks.

That's more than I earn in a year. Yesterday I'd have done this gig for fifty bucks. Now I had two grand in front of me.

And I still wasn't sure.

Why the hell not?

Because I had a deal with Gray, that's why. And because... because Lisa Borden.

When she looked at me with disappointment in those baby blues I felt like a heel. The worst kind of heel.

'I don't know,' I answered. 'I got a deal with my client. If he owns the bird, I need to hand it over to him.'

'If?' That was Lisa Borden talking. I still heard the disappointment there.

'Like you said,' I answered, 'can he own it if it's stolen from a tomb or from the country it came from?'

'If he *doesn't* own it?'

'Then I got no deal with him because I ain't handling hot goods.' I sighed and blew off the best deal of my life. 'I guess that means they just offered *you* two grand for the bird.'

I couldn't believe I just turned away from two grand.

Neither could Lisa Borden.

Two grand.

You could almost buy a house with two thousand bucks. Hell,

you were halfway to owning a real nice place. With two grand you were on your way to Easy Street.

Why the Hell had I handed it over to a dame I hardly knew? Because she was a looker?

Because it was the right thing to do? If Gray didn't own it, I really didn't have a right to hand it to him.

And this crew opposite? Who were they? They laughed and joked but they were serious underneath. They weren't amateurs. The broad playing the Warrior Queen was a fighter all right. She had kicked my ass without breaking sweat. They all had English accents and the English still had big influence in Egypt, right? A Protectorate or something? My guess was that they were some kind of official undercover bunch for the Brits. If I was right, I would rather they got the bird instead of Gray, even if it cost me my other two-fifty. He could whistle for getting the advance back.

I looked hard at Lisa Borden. It was in her hands now. She looked like I'd stuck a live electric cable in her palm.

'So,' I said, 'what do you think?'

'I... I...' she struggled for words. 'I don't know. I don't know who your boss is and I don't know who these people are.'

'Can you tell us that?'

The Warrior Queen shook her head. 'No.'

'Yes,' the other actress said. The one who couldn't sing. She reached under the table and pulled out four envelopes. She distributed them to her group. They each took a pass out of their envelopes.

'Where did you get these?' the guy – Ibrahim – asked.

'I left them here earlier,' the non-singer said. 'Just remind me later that I need to do it earlier.'

I didn't understand a word, but they quickly showed their passes before stashing them. They sure looked official to me. **United Kingdom of Great Britain and Northern Ireland, Special Intelligence Service, Department Without Portfolio.**

I'd been right. 'You're all spooks.'

'Military Intelligence,' the non-singer agreed.

'Which makes this meeting completely confidential,' the attractive, slightly older woman – Helena according to her ID – said carefully.

Erimem, the Queen, piped in. 'If you share this information about us, you may not live to regret it.'

'Hey,' I protested, 'aren't we friends?'

'We will be,' Helena said.

I didn't have a clue what that meant. 'What?'

Queenie was getting impatient. 'This is irrelevant. We need the statue. Will you give it to us?'

Lisa answered that with a question to me. 'What happens if you don't give it to your boss?'

I shrugged. 'He's ticked off.'

Lisa Borden wasn't put off by a wise-ass line. 'Meaning?'

Just this once I went with a totally honest answer. 'I don't know. I don't know if he had muscle on call.'

'So he might kill you?'

'I doubt it. Better than him have tried.' Yeah, that was balls and BS and nobody was buying it.

Lisa kept digging. 'But you will lose money.'

'Some,' I admitted. 'But I'll have enough to skip town for a few weeks till the heat dies down some.'

Lisa Borden thought long and hard. She was weighing it all.

'I'll give you the statue,' she said to the Brits, 'but it'll cost you three thousand bucks. Half for me, half for Stone.'

'Three thousand?' Helena shrugged. 'Fair enough.'

'Really?' Lisa sounded shocked. 'Damn, I should have asked for four thousand.'

The non-singer sighed loudly. 'Why don't we call it five grand and everybody's happy?'

'Hey,' the guy protested. So he was the money man, huh?

Queen Erimem just nodded. 'Call it five thousand, then. I really do not care.'

'Five grand?' Pretty sure I squeaked that like Mickey Mouse.

Lisa shut me up. 'We'll take it.'

Damn right we would take it.

It still didn't feel right, though. Five grand to stop Hitler getting a statue that turned people into what? Vampires? Monsters like Frankenstein? Nobody believed in that hokum, did they?

Somebody believed enough to pay five grand.

I wasn't going to think about that too much. I knew

something was wrong. I felt it in my gut. But that kind of money made it easier to ignore the gut-ache. I'd ignored morals for less.

'Do you have the statue?' the older woman, Helena, asked.

'You got the cash?' I shot back.

She held her hands wide. 'Fair point. I'll get the money this afternoon.'

'Can you get the statue today?' Queenie asked Lisa.

Lisa grimaced. She wasn't sure. 'If I can talk to the guy who's cleaning it.'

'If you can't?'

'It'll be tomorrow.'

Queenie didn't care for that. 'I don't like the idea of leaving something so dangerous lying around.'

The sister agreed. 'Especially if the goosestep gang are after it as well.'

Queenie gave it some thought. 'It is useless without the correct incantation, I suppose...'

Her sister prodded her arm. 'You never mentioned an incantation before.'

'Didn't I?'

Another prod from the can't-sing sister. 'Remember to tell us stuff, love.'

Queenie didn't look too happy. 'It should be safe, but it would be safer to get it back to the villa today.'

'I'll try to get it for you,' Lisa promised.

'Hey, kids.'

Some guy I didn't recognize had joined the table. I'd seen him on the lot but I didn't know who he was.

'Mr Reed,' Helena said.

That explained it. He had to be Carson Reed, the director.

'Why are you sitting here out of the way? The rest of the talent is over there.' He waved a hand, dismissing Lisa. 'No offence, Laura.'

'Lisa,' she corrected him.

'Yeah. Whatever.'

I wanted to punch him for that.

The sister looked across at the talent-table. 'And I don't see our leading man. What's he getting fixed? The rug or the corset?'

Reed didn't like that. 'Repeat that and you'll never work in this town again.'

Lisa chimed in. 'Besides, everybody knows he likes vodka for lunch.'

The pointed finger switched to aiming at her. 'You repeat that and I'll fire you.' Reed turned back to Queenie. 'So why are you with the help?'

I'm gonna give Queenie credit. She really didn't like the way Reed talked down to Lisa and me. The ass-hole didn't even know I didn't work for him. 'Because she did good work and we wished to tell her so.'

Reed snorted. 'Damn, you really are new here. Look, you're in the movies. You're expected to act a certain way. Like tonight, there's a bash at the *Tropicana*. You and your sister need to be there. Especially you.' He looked at the non-singer. 'Your sister... optional extra.'

Sis didn't take kindly to that. 'Thanks, I *am* still here.'

Reed didn't care. 'But you're not the star.'

'You want us at a party tonight?' Queenie said.

'Yeah, it's for some bigwig over at Warners. Jack's throwing him a party. Lots of photographers. That means you're going.'

Queenie thought then answered. 'No.'

Helena pushed herself between Queenie and Reed, 'And by no she means yes.'

'No, I don't.'

Helena didn't look at her friend. 'Yes, you do. It's part of the game. She'll be there. We all will.'

'Okay,' Reed grunted.

'All six of us.' Helena indicated Lisa and me.

'Six? Hey, we don't take the help.'

'To tell the truth,' Lisa said sourly. 'I'm never that much help.'

'But tonight she is coming,' Queenie said, 'or I will stay at home.'

Reed didn't look happy. Good. He was behaving like an ass. 'Oh great, I hired a diva.'

Queenie shook her head. 'No, just someone who would like a few familiar faces around.'

'Oh. I get you.' She had played him but good. She was saying she was nervous and a friendly face would make it all easier.

'You got something swanky to wear?' Reed asked Lisa.

She didn't look happy. 'Nobody's asking if I want to go?'

Like Reed cared about that. 'Don't be dumb. So, you got something swanky?'

'If I don't?'

'Get something.'

'On what I get paid here?'

Reed just looked sour. 'You work next to a costume department. Work it out. We'll send a car for you.'

'Great,' Lisa grouched.

'Not for you.'

'You went to charm school, didn't you?' Helena said. 'What a pity it was shut.'

Reed shrugged. 'Like Hitch said, actors are cattle.' That was the end for him. He'd said what he had to and he was gone.

'Why did you do that?' Lisa asked Helena.

I answered. 'Because they want to keep their eyes on us.'

Helena was up-front and honest. 'Yes.'

'That's not very friendly,' I said.

'We're taking you to a party,' Sis said. 'What could be more friendly that that?'

Lisa still had her hand on mine. She squeezed to get my attention. 'Five grand's a big investment, Stone. For that I guess I'd be wary, too.'

I couldn't disagree with that but I still didn't like it. Being told what to do made my gut ache. 'Okay,' I said, 'I guess we're going to a party.'

CHAPTER TEN

Food at the studio canteen? Not as good as the bacon rolls I dish up at the café. It was bacon that broke my vegetarianism. I tried to resist but grilling rashers day after day wore me down.

I'm digressing.

It was kind of weird seeing everybody on edge – especially now we knew that Nazis were responsible for the attack. I couldn't shake the feeling that we should share the info with the cops. But that would ask too many questions. It would certainly stop us from getting the statue. So we kept our lips glued.

Lunch was cut short. Carson insisted on introducing us to everybody important. Well, he introduced Erimem. He mentioned me as the sister and just ignore Ibrahim and Helena. As for Lisa Borden and her hulking boyfriend/bodyguard/ whatever-they-were, they got dropped like yesterday's garbage.

(I told you – speaking like this is addictive!)

We met the stars of the various movies. The guys looked at us wondering how quick they'd get us into bed. The women wondered if we were competition. Directors looked at us like we were on show at a cattle markets. Writers started talking about the sisters angle. Everybody else ate lunch.

Back on set, it was my first scene. First? Hell, damn near my only scene.

I was in the background doing some miming a song while Erimem had a scene with John Buttler and Peter Arthur.

Buttler was a bit shaky on his lines. Shaky on his legs, too. I think he'd taken too much vodka flavoured medicine. Credit where it's due, though. He's was Oliver Reed-standard whammo and still managed to be word perfect on his third take. Peter Arthur just hit his marks, knew his lines and had energy.

Carson Reed liked that. Before every take he shouted 'Energy, energy, energy.' It's every bit as annoying as it sounds. It worked, though. He got everybody buzzing.

Scenes got recorded out of order. It took me a second to work out that Buttler had more lines this morning. Peter and Goldie had most of the dialogue in the afternoon. Carson Reed knew his star was a booze-hound and worked round it.

I was in the background miming my lungs out for the scenes. I'm a pretty damn good singer when I'm miming.

The movie was shot a lot quicker than I expected. I've seen documentaries. Judi Dench complaining she's sitting about all day waiting for things to get set up. Not on this set. The turnaround was instant. One shot was done and everybody just assembled and moved onto the next one. Five minutes later the camera was rolling again. It really was fast.

I'm not saying the studio were cheap. But they were cheap. Scripts were written so they went back to the same location. That meant the same sets were used and reused. Less money spent on sets, less time spent building different sets. It made sense. It made the process feel kind of like a factory, too.

Erimem wasn't in every scene I was. She was in the stuff filmed early in the day. Later on we did a scene before she turned up in the movie. Goldie Raines (I can't keep calling her that) being introduced by Peter Arthur's character to his boss, played by John Buttler. I wondered if they set scenes in nightclubs and bars to make up for him being sauced. I got my backside kicked for moving too suggestively in one take.

It's good to know I've still got it.

CHAPTER ELEVEN

It felt weird being back at Lisa Borden's work table. The place should have been busy. It wasn't. Anybody who would be there was dead or in hospital. People came and went but Lisa was the only one really working there. She moved from table to table, covering for everybody. She worked her ass off.

Honest truth is I didn't know why I was there.

Two and a half grand? That's a lot of reasons.

So I had to keep Lisa safe till she got the bird, right?

Yeah. Right.

I was there because I wanted to be. Because I thought Lisa Borden wanted me to be there.

I told myself I owed her. She was an innocent in this.

What about me? Was I an innocent? It was a long time since I was innocent of everything. With Nazis, British spies, attacks on people going about their work... and Mr Gray. I'd been thinking about him. I always knew he was trouble. The money was a giveaway. I was out of my league. I was pretty sure I'd have to get out of town for a while after we handed over the bird. I told Lisa Borden she should do the same.

'You asking me to elope, Stone?' she asked.

'If I did you'd say no.'

'Suddenly you're psychic.'

That was sign I needed to put the full stop to that conversation with her.

'Classy women confuse me.'

'That's the idea.'

A few times I caught Lisa Borden glancing at her colleague's tables. Where here friends should have been. This teasing, this sass... it was cover for how she felt about them. So, I went along with it. It kept her calm. It got me nearer the dough. I told myself that was the reason I stuck around and played along.

Even I knew I was a lying son-of-a-bitch.

Lisa picked out an outfit in the middle of the afternoon. She was quick about it. I always had a beef with dames who take an age over their clothes. Same with guys who take an age with clothes. One of the first guys I worked with on the job took longer to dress than anybody I ever met. Why do we always just say it's dames?

When she came back she'd picked out a suit for me. I guessed that meant she didn't think much of the one I was wearing.

We got lucky before we left for that damn party. The cops moved out. The guy who had the statue said we could pick it up.

I guessed Lisa wasn't greedy. She wasn't the type. But even she was pulled to this kind of money. Anybody would be.

We made our way to pick up the statue. The door was open and we hurried through to the workshop.

Stupid move.

I should have been more careful.

By the time I registered the two security guys on the floor bleeding out it was too late. There were four guys. Jesus, they even *looked* like Nazis. Soulless eyes and a superior sneer on every face. Two of them were beating the hell out of a forty-ish guy. One of them held the statue. They had the bird but they were beating this guy anyway. Yeah, they were Nazis all right.

Instinct already had my pistol in my hand. 'Hold it right there.'

I hadn't noticed that two of the Nazis held pistols low. They opened fire. I grabbed Lisa and pulled her behind a heavy wooden work-bench. Bullets sang around us. They spat chucks out of the bench. Splinters that could kill as easy as the bullets if they hit you the wrong way.

I fired back. I just loosed one shot to hold them at bay. I got lucky. I heard one of them scream. Not a dying scream. Just a hurt one.

'Keep down,' I told Lisa.

She was scared but she still had her wits. 'What can I do?'

There was no point in lying. 'Not much. One of them is hurt but that doesn't help us much.'

I let loose another shot. This time nobody screamed.

We were sunk.

They had more guns. They had better cover. They had to pass us to get out.

And god-dammit, they had the bird. They had our five grand and there wasn't a damn thing I could do about it.

They were moving closer. They guy on the left sounded nearest. I fired blind around the corner. He screamed.

I didn't wait. I threw myself around the side of the bench. In three steps I was on him. He was shot in the gut. It was bad. I made it worse by driving my fist at the bullet wound. His blood covered my hand. I ignored it. Punched him again. He dropped his Luger. I scooped it up in my bloodied hand. Now I had a pistol in either hand. Old West style. I fired once with each pistol. I clipped one Nazi in the shoulder.

We had a chance.

'Enough, Mr Stone.'

I turned. One of the Nazis had Lisa Borden. He held her in front of him, his Luger aimed at her.

She looked terrified.

'Put the weapons down or I will kill Fraulein Borden.'

He wasn't kidding. He looked like he'd enjoy killing her too.

'How do I know you won't just kill her anyway?'

'You don't.'

'And how do I know you won't just kill me?'

'You don't.' Damn, this guy didn't have much vocabulary.

He didn't have much to make me trust him either.

'You need to keep one of us alive,' I said.

An eyebrow lifted on Fritzy, just a quarter inch. 'And why is that?'

'Because there's an incantation goes with that little chicken you stole,' I said. 'The juju your boss is after don't work without it.'

Fritzy looked more interested. 'You know more than I thought, Herr Stone. Tell me more.'

'If I tell you that, I'm dead,' I said. 'You got no use for me after I tell you.'

'Perhaps I have no use for you at all. I am sure I could make Miss Borden speak.'

'I'm sure you could,' I said.

'I won't talk,' Lisa Borden said.

I believed her. They could rip her arm out and she would tell these sons-of-bitches nothing. They'd enjoy trying to make her talk, though.

'I know you won't talk,' I said. My pistol moved slightly to the side. Instead of aiming at Fritzy's chest I was aiming at Lisa Borden. 'Sorry, kid. You're a swell dame and acting up like I was taken with you was fun.' I shrugged. 'But you know how it is in this town. Everything's an act, even you and me. I guess I have to cancel our date tonight.'

The pistol twitched and then jerked in my hand. The single shot seemed louder than when there had been a dozen.

Lisa Borden spun away from the German and crashed into a stand of jars and beakers holding liquids. She looked at me, eyes wide in shock before her knees buckled and she dropped face down on the floor.

'I told ya, kid,' I said sadly, 'I ain't no hero.'

Ever had a Nazi look at you with disgust? It doesn't get much lower than that.

I threw the pistols away. Mine skidded along the floor and nudged against Lisa Borden's still corpse. Red was leaking from under her body.

I looked at Fritzy, he seemed to be the leader of this goon patrol. 'Okay, Fritzy, now what?'

I got the question out before something slugged me on the back of the head and the world started spinning. I was kind of aware that they were dragging me out. I remember thinking it was ruining the shine on my shoes. I tried to move but couldn't, tried to speak but couldn't. I couldn't even raise a groan.

They threw me into the trunk of their car. It wasn't a new deal for me. I felt unconsciousness coming. My last thought was that I hoped somehow Lisa Borden would be able to forgive me for killing her.

I was relieved when I felt it all go black.

* * *

Nothing wakes you up quite like a bright light in your eyes and a slug to the mouth. These Nazis sure knew how to do it old school.

I blinked against the light. We were in a motel of some kind. That *some kind* was not the good kind.

They had a lamp aimed straight in my kisser. My eyeballs ached as much as the back of my skull where they'd cracked me.

Ignore it, Stone. Ignore it. Take in the surroundings. Be professional.

Fritzy was in front of me on one side of the lamp. One of his goons was on the other side of it. What about the other two? I saw one lying on a bed. He was being tended by one who had a bandage round his upper arm. I was glad to see blood seeping through the bandage. He would live but it would hurt. I wasn't sure his buddy would make it without a hospital. Hell I didn't think he'd make it *with* a hospital. They always used to tell us that gut-shot was a bad way to go.

Fritzy got straight to the point. 'Herr Stone, you will tell us about the incantation.'

'Don't I even get a "Hi, how are ya?" or maybe a cup of Joe?'

Wise-ass is the only schtick I got.

Fritzy didn't like it much. 'Listen carefully, Herr Stone. You have shot one of my men in the stomach. He is likely to die. You have injured another of my men. I would kill you for either of those acts. I would also kill you for shooting Fraulein Borden. We do not tolerate cowards in my country.'

'Or Jews, I answered, 'or gypsies, coloureds, guys who like guys... you got a long list of people you don't tolerate and some vicious ways of showing it.'

I thought that was it. I'd pushed too hard.

Fritzy was angry all right – but he controlled it. 'I am glad you know so much about us, Herr Stone. It will save me the trouble of persuading you that we are serious.'

I thought of Red and her colleagues. 'Killing those unarmed civilians at the studio told me that.'

'And you killed a woman who had some affection for you, Herr Stone. You are no better than us.'

I couldn't argue with that. 'Okay,' I conceded. 'What do you want?'

'Exactly what you promised, Herr Stone. The complete incantation. We only have part of it. We must have it all.'

So, they didn't have it all. That was something for me to work with. Not much but something. 'Do you have it in the original or translated?' I asked.

'Transcribed phonetically,' Fritzy answered.

I was impressed. He knew big words in more than one language.

'That's good,' I lied, 'that's how I got it too. Show me how far into it you got.'

'You are keen to help us.'

Fritzy didn't trust me. He was right. I'm a hell of a liar. Just ask Lisa Borden.

'I'm eager to stay alive,' I said. 'I do what you want, and you let me go?'

It was Fritzy's turn to lie. 'Of course.'

I nodded. 'Then show me what you have, so I can get out and you can get your friend there to a hospital or wherever you're going to get him fixed up.'

Fritzy glanced at his colleague. The man had drifted into unconsciousness. 'He is not coming with us when we leave. You know as well as I do that if he was to survive he would already have to be in a hospital.'

Honestly? I didn't care. 'Saving lives was never my thing. So, we going to get this done?'

Fritzy led me to a table and put two sheets of paper on it. 'This is what we have. We believe there are the equivalent of four lines missing.'

It looked like random letters scattered on the page. I didn't recognize a single word. Hell, there was no way I could. I didn't know what I was looking at. I didn't recognize any of the words that were written out. How could I? All I knew about the incantation was what Queenie had said. I didn't buy this magic guff but Hitler obviously did – and that meant his goons did, too. That gave me a chance. A chance to stay alive, a chance to get away from these thugs and a chance to steal the bird. A chance to land five grand.

I leaned over the table, looking at the sheets of paper. I nodded my head in a rhythm and mouthed the words. Yeah, it was baloney but it looked like I knew what I was doing. I was reading the words like I knew them. Nodded my head like I knew the cadence.

I noted where they all were. Gut-Shot was on the bed tended by Shoulder Injury. Fritzy and the one with dead eyes were the two I really had to worry about. They were behind and on opposite sides of me. Fritzy was on the right and closer. Dead Eyes stood further back on the left. I needed to move them. Get them closer.

'You got a pen and spare paper?' I asked.

Fritzy nodded for Dead Eyes to bring a pen and paper. He slammed them down in front of me and stepped back. Yeah, but not as far back as he had been before.

Almost close enough for me to get the jump on him.

Almost but not quite.

Fritzy was getting antsy. 'What is the delay?'

'You want it quick or you want it right?' I asked.

'I want both!'

Dead Eyes stepped closer. He was a threat. That was okay. He was close enough now. I just needed Fritzy to take a step closer and to relax his guard.

I went back to the nodding and mouthing words.

I had to fill some kinda baloney in.

What the hell could I write?

'You're missing the part where everyone joins the incantation. Some kind of summoning thing, I think.' I shrugged. 'I don't know.'

Fritzy came half a step closer. 'Write.'

I did as I was told.

Ahad Ahad A Hadi O.
(All) Ahad Ahad A Hadi O.
Ahi Dehi Dehi De Hi.
(All) Ahi Dehi Dehi De Hi.
Scoo Di Lee Vu
Scoo Di Lee Vu
Scoo Di Lee Vu Di Lee Vu
(All) Scoo Di Lee Vu Di Lee Vu

I'd started to sweat. If they made sense of what I wrote I was dead for sure. I guessed they wouldn't. I hoped they wouldn't.

'Okay,' I said. 'I think it's done.'

Fritzy and Dead Eyes both took a step closer to read what I wrote. I'd slipped the pen to my left hand. I swung it hard and high. It went deep into Dead Eyes' neck. It wasn't fatal but it did enough damage. Fritzy was surprised just long enough for me to scoop up the bird and lay it across his jaw but hard. He went down. Blood and teeth sprayed the floor.

I grabbed the papers and ran. I still held onto the statue. This baby was still worth five grand.

I jerked the door open and kept running. If I could steal their car I was home free. If not... well, I could improvise. I knew more low-life ways to hide that most. Benefit of being a cop.

Damn. I was on a landing. That meant stairs. Stairs were exposed.

I had no choice. I ran. One step at a time was quickest. More than that, you risk losing your balance and slow to compensate. Just keep the feet moving.

I made it to the ground floor hall. The front door was ahead.
Run, dammit!

I grabbed the handle and pulled.

It sounded like an explosion behind me and the door disintegrated in a hail of splinters.

The Nazi with the injured shoulder was on the stairs. He had a machine gun aimed at me. He wanted the bird and the papers back but the look on his face said he'd settle for taking them in pieces if I tried to run.
Damn it.

Could I risk it? Was there another way out? A door into an apartment maybe?

Another voice. Slurred like the guy speaking was gargling with an open mouth.

Or speaking with a mouth full of blood and broken teeth after somebody slugged him in the kisser with a statue. He sprayed red froth as he spoke. It spattered the pistol he was aiming at me.

'Stupid, Herr Stone. Stupid. Bring our property back.'

I looked at the door again.
Could I get through?

Fritzy knew what I was thinking. 'Karl, if Herr Stone tries to escape you will empty your machine gun into his head.' He turned away. 'I trust that is clear, Herr Stone. Karl, if Herr Stone does not come back up the stairs in twenty seconds, kill him.'

Karl was bleeding from his injured shoulder. I could see the stain had spread. He was still more than capable to blowing me to hell.

I had no choice. 'All right. You win.'

I climbed the stairs slowly. Karl kept his eyes on me. They were wise to me now. He gave me no chance to get near enough to jump him.

'The statue and the papers, Herr Stone.' Fritzy held his hands out in demand and I handed them back. I didn't have a choice.

Fritzy took the bird and the papers.

Two seconds later I was on my back, a screaming pain from my legs blocking everything else from my head. I saw the Dead Eyes had some kind of baton in his hand. Then he had it on the back of my legs again. Then my ribs. Karl joined in the fun. While Dead Eyes aped Gene Krupa playing a drum solo cracking my ribs, Karl added some hefty kicks. I tried to cover up but it was no good. Dead Eyes had a handkerchief tied around his neck. It was crimson and blood still poured onto his shirt. Maybe if he kept hitting me he'd bleed to death.

'Enough!' Fritzy's voice stopped the beating. The pain of the fresh blows stopped. The agony from the damage they had already done kicked in to make up for it. I tried to push myself upright. Not a chance.

'Gather here,' Fritzy said. 'The Falcon is more important than the American.'

I hurt too much to be offended.

I tried to push myself up again. It still just hurt too damn much.

I heard them light candles and arrange papers and the statue.

The chant started. Fritzy was reading. I wasn't surprised. Son-of-a-bitch had an ego. I wondered how he would feel when absolutely nothing happened. This talk of magic was as cracked as their goofy little Fuhrer. They were going to feel like clowns when they clicked there was no magic and that I'd never even heard that damn incantation.

Yeah. That would probably be when they killed me.

At least I'd die laughing. I was going out on a hell of a rip.

Fritzy was giving the incantation everything. He must have really bought a big helping of Hitler's baloney.

I guessed I was bleeding inside. I could hear a sort of pounding sound. The way you sometimes think you hear your blood pulse through you when your head is on the pillow. I might get lucky and die before they could kill me. A last act of spite.

It wasn't my blood I could hear. I didn't know what the hell it was. A huge heartbeat? Some damn thing. I forced my eyes open, made myself look at the Nazis.

The bird was glowing. It was changing colour. Black was turning gold.

I had to be dreaming. A last hallucination before I died?

No. The damn thing really was glowing. Patches of gold spreading, reaching out, joining with others and filling the gap. Its eyes burned red. Red and alive?

The pulsing was coming from the bird. I saw them. The air shimmered. It actually shook.

It's a strange moment when you realise that something you dismissed as baloney turns out to be real. Somehow it gives you energy.

I pushed myself up onto my hands and knees. The incantation was bringing some life to this bird. The Nazis' skin reflected the gold. Not just gold... was there green in there? Wisps of purple, too.

'Ahad Ahad A Hadi O.'

The light pulsed an angry purple. Tendrils shot out and blasted a hole in the wall.

They carried on the incantation.

They were chanting what I had added – and what I'd added was anything but ancient Egyptian.

Yeah. The lines I'd added to the incantation? Cab Calloway's scatting from *Minnie the Moocher*. It was all I'd been able to think of.

'Ahad Ahad A Hadi O'

More blasts of purple lightning ripped the room. One tore into Gut-Shot, the Nazi dying on the bed. He writhed and tried to scream. Purple lightning shot out of his nose and mouth.

It was time to get the hell out of Dodge.

I just about staggered to my feet and lurched out of the room. I lost my footing on the stairs and rolled down, out of control. Hitting the edges of those stairs on the way down hurt worse that the beating.

I couldn't stop.

Stand up, you dumb son-of-a-bitch and keep moving.

The gunfire had shredded the door around the lock. I just crashed through, out into the street. I kept moving. It was a quiet part of town. Too quiet. Derelict was more accurate. No traffic for me to flag down. No people to help me.

Keep moving.

There was an alley. I'd be able to see the house from there.

The windows glowed gold, green and purple. It was like a thunderstorm was happening in there. Bolts of lightning blasted through the outer walls, smashed the windows out. I heard the Nazis' screams. One of them staggered to the window and was impaled on a flash of lightning. He glowed golden green and then dropped from sight.

I had no sympathy for those bastards but that was no way to die.

The light dimmed. I guessed that was it. Whatever that thing was, it had killed them.

Got to admit, I did think I could try to go back in. I could still score five grand for the bird.

There was movement at the door.

What the hell?

The Nazis were walking out. All of them. All four of them. Even Gut-Shot.

They moved with stiff walks, unnatural walks. Jeez, what the hell had happened to their skin? It was kinda green, and blistered but it looked *decayed.* Their eyes were... they looked dead but somehow still moved.

A bum shambled along the street towards them. I should have shouted something but it was too late. They were on him, tearing at him, clawing at him. He screamed and dropped to the ground. They beat him and ripped at him some more The Nazis shambled off along the street. I started to follow then stopped. The bum they had attacked was moving. He was still alive.

Alive?

I was close enough to see his face changing colour, taking on that same dead colour as the Nazis. The flesh started flaking even in those seconds. Then he was on his feet and following the Nazis.

I hurried after them all as fast as I could.

The way the Nazis had attacked him I was sure he was dead.

If he was, the dead were walking in Hollywood.

CHAPTER TWELVE

So we went to a Hollywood party at a swanky nightclub. Oh, hell, yeah we did. This was a good one, too. The *Tropicana*. You know what? Drinks at *Club Tropicana* really were free. Wham told the truth all those years ago.

We were dolled-up and looking good. Pretty much everywhere you looked there was glamour. Real, proper Hollywood glamour. And we were getting introduced to everyone. Olivia deHavilland, Paulette Goddard, Hedy Lamarr (*"Not Hedley! Not Hedley! Don't say Hedley!"*), Carole Lombard, Bette Davis... plus a couple of dozen faces I'd need a minute or two to name. Photographers were snapping pictures of Ginger Rogers and Fred Astaire. I think I have a crush on Ginger Rogers. Spencer Tracey and Katherine Hepburn were avoiding each other so obviously they had to have something going on between them. As for the men? John Wayne was a head taller than most. Clarke Cable was charming, Jimmy Stewart was as Jimmy Stewart you thought he would be and Errol Flynn had charm but didn't hide that he was staring at my tits. I didn't hide that he was out of luck. Basil Rathbone apologised for him. You can always trust Sherlock Holmes.

Erimem and I had been introduced to all of these celebs. We weren't the stars of the evening but we were new, we were a curiosity and we got a fair bit of interest from producers and the press. Somewhere there are pictures of us with all of these big names.

I want those pictures.

The party was really interesting. Fun and business making a mix of genuine friendships and some nasty politics.

You know who I liked that I didn't expect to? John Wayne. I'd heard stories of him being crazy right-wing. He was just really nice to Erimem and me. The Duke chilling and spending time with a lady of colour and LGBT-me and he was just really nice.

'I guess you two got an interesting story,' he said, 'but I won't pry.'

'It is no secret that we have different mothers,' Erimem answered.

That was enough explanation for him. 'But you got each other,' he said seriously. 'This town can be tough. It can be mean. Stick together. Look after each other and you'll be fine.'

'We are best friends as well as sisters,' Erimem said. That touched me. It really did.

Duke was being called over by a producer. He gave a warm smile. 'Maybe we'll work together one of these days.'

'I hope so,' Erimem nodded.

The champagne was good, the chat was interesting and meeting genuine movie icons *en masse* like this was just extraordinary. I was gutted that David Niven wasn't there. I always liked him in old movies. But he was back in Blighty, in uniform and doing his bit in the war.

You know what else was odd about meeting these celebs? How normal they were. They all had little problems and quirks. There were niggly little arguments between couples that they tried to hide and keep quiet. Some of the celebs were playing pranks on each other and others were gossiping. It was incredibly *normal*.

I bloody loved it!

I knew the fun was going to end when Ibrahim hurried across. His face said something had happened. 'We have a problem.'

I tried to stay jovial. 'What a cheek. I've only had one glass of champers.'

He didn't smile. Okay, that meant it really was serious. Erimem had spotted the serious face and joined us.

'What is it?' she asked.

Ibrahim nodded towards a side door. 'Come with me.'

We followed him through the door into a corridor and along to a little office.

Helena was in doctor mode, tending to a blonde woman. 'Eyes left. Now to the right. Keep your eyes on my finger, watch it move back and forward. You're fine. No concussion.'

Helena moved and we saw her patient.

Lisa Borden was covered in blood. He was wearing the same clothes she had been wearing that afternoon, but now the front of her blouse and cardigan were crimson. She had a bruise on her temple and a few cuts here and there.

'What happened?' Erimem demanded.

Lisa looked up. 'They have Stone.'

'Who has?' Erimem asked.

'The Nazis,' Lisa answered quickly. 'They took the statue and they took Stone.'

Erimem stiffened. 'These Nazis have the Falcon?'

Lisa confirmed that. 'And Stone.'

'Why would they take Stone?' I asked.

Lisa answered, sharp and agitated. 'He told them the statue was useless without the incantation – just like you said – and he told them he knew the incantation.'

'That was bloody stupid of him,' I said. 'Bloody brave too.'

Lisa looked at me wryly. 'You think he's going to give up on that much money?'

'Why didn't they take you too?' Ibrahim asked.

'Stone shot me,' Lisa said. 'At least he pretended to so they wouldn't torture me, I guess. He missed me but I played like he got me. When I went down I grabbed a sachet of red dye.' She plucked at her blouse. 'I don't know how I'll explain this to Mom.'

Helena patted her arm comfortingly. 'At least you're here to do the explaining.'

'Where did they take him?' Erimem asked.

Lisa shook her head. 'I don't know. We didn't have time to talk it out. He talked about Hollywood being fake, about him liking me being fake... but I saw he wasn't aiming straight at me.'

'He let himself be taken prisoner to save you,' Helena told her. 'I think that means the liking you is genuine.'

Lisa nodded. Her affection for the detective was real, too.

'Can you help me? I need to find him.'

'I need to find that statue,' Erimem said.

Lisa didn't care. 'Stone is more important.'

'To you. To the rest of the world... no.' That was it. The switch was flicked. Happy, playful, party Erimem was gone. The warrior, the general had taken her place. Stone was now just part of a battle she had to plan. If he was a casualty of war... so be it. 'Can you think of a way to track these Nazis?' she asked me.

'Not that I can think of. I don't have a loony-detector. They have to have a base somewhere.'

'And now they have the Falcon they will try to leave?' Ibrahim asked.

Erimem nodded. 'Possibly. How would they leave?' she asked Lisa.

There wasn't any real answer to that. 'There are a lot of ways out of this city.'

'Road, train, plane, boat...' Helena said thoughtfully. 'We can't cover them all.'

'They came in by flying boat,' Lisa said. 'Stone told me.'

'We can check to see if one's leaving today,' Helena said. 'I'll get on to that.'

I sighed. 'Looks like the party's over.'

We hurried back out into the party.

Carson Reed was looking for us. 'Where the hell have you been? I got Michael Curtiz over there. He's interested in you for a nightclub flick he's attached to. Not a big role. A dame who works at a nightclub in Casabl...'

Erimem pushed past Carson. 'We have to leave now,' she said.

The director choked, 'What?'

'Lisa's boyfriend has been attacked,' I explained.

'He's not my boyfriend.' Lisa said it automatically. She didn't believe it.

Carson Reed just stared at Lisa's crimson-stained clothes.

Erimem just wanted to keep on moving. 'But he has been attacked and we must help him.'

Reed was only worried about his movie. 'I'll get the cops onto it. It's their job.'

Helena pushed past him. 'What would have happened to you

if we had waited for the cops?'

'That was different.'

'How?' I asked.

'It was *me*.'

'That's what I thought.' I shrugged. 'Say sorry to the Duke for us.'

That was as far as we got.

Somebody screamed from the door.

Then somebody else. Suddenly there were dozens of people screaming and running.

'What the hell?' That was Reed.

A gang of men and women, all of them with dull green, decaying skin and dead eyes were pushing their way into the party, attacking anyone they could grab, clawing at them, tearing at them.

Lisa Borden was pointing. 'There. Those are the Nazis.'

'Oh, bollocks,' I muttered. 'Nazi zombies? *Really?*'

CHAPTER THIRTEEN

I'd followed the Nazis through LA for over an hour. I couldn't move fast but they weren't in a hurry. They attacked everybody they met. A minute later, the victim joined them. Their numbers just kept growing. There were about fifty by the time I realized where they were going.

The Tropicana Nightclub. Where the party was being held.

I was struggling to keep up. I'd coughed up some blood. I guessed that wasn't a good sign. The second cough convinced me I had serious internal damage.

I kept going anyway. Hell, if I was going to die I might as well take in the show, right?

Fritzy's undead army just swarmed the parking lot. They attacked reporters and valets, smashing them with their fists. They ripped at them with fingers bent into claws. They even bit and tore them with their teeth. It was chaos. A snapper fired off a photograph. The bulb flared in one of the walking dead's faces. It made the thing stagger away. It wasn't much of a win. Others were on the photographer and a minute later he was swarming through the door after them.

Why had they come to this club? They hadn't come by accident. Why had they made a bee-line for this place?

They weren't even on the guest list.

Damn. That left-field gag made me realize I was starting to lose focus.

Concentrate, you dumb bastard. Concentrate.

Why would they come here? Queenie and her entourage were all to be here. It could be them?

A thought came to me. One that scared me.

What if Lisa Borden had come to them for help? What if Lisa was in there? What if she wound up like these others? Dead but walking.

I knew I was in trouble. I guessed I probably had a damaged lung. I was probably bleeding into it. One of the guys at my first station house drowned by bleeding into his own lungs after he took a beating. Yeah, that hadn't been a great way to go. Better to go down fighting.

I pulled my strength together and headed for the club. One of the swanky automobiles had a tire iron clipped to the back. I took that and started swinging.

It was time to make the dead hurt.

CHAPTER FOURTEEN

It's like a crappy 1980s movie title: *Nazi Zombies in Hollywood*.

Yep, pretty sure somebody must have made that movie sometime. I guessed it would be about as much fun as living it as watching it.

Everybody sensible was running away from the zombies fighting their way into the club.

So Erimem was pushing her way towards them for a closer look.

'Look at the skin,' she said. 'They must have somehow activated the Falcon.'

I wasn't much smarter than Erimem. I was right behind her. 'How?'

'I don't know.' She looked around. 'We must get these people away from these... what did you call them? Zumbas?'

'Zombies.'

'Yes. We must get them away from the zombies.'

We were lucky. The main area of the club was up eighteen very swanky steps from the entrance. That was the only way up to the actual party level.

Erimem was already issuing orders. 'Block the stairs.'

'What about the people down there?' a blonde actress (don't ask me which one) asked.

Erimem was already hurling chairs onto the steps. 'Look at them,' she snapped. 'When they fall, they rise again as our foes. They are lost.'

Blondie wailed. I just pushed her towards a group of people.

They could deal with her.

'We need to use tables,' I said.

Erimem nodded. We started heaving a table towards the stairs. It was just too heavy for us to move quickly. Ibrahim and Helena joined us and we toppled a big shiny and probably expensive table onto the steps. It wasn't a barricade on its own but it was a start.

The Hollywood crowd just stood and watched.

That's not Erimem's style. 'What are you waiting for?' she roared. 'Block the stairs.'

Jimmy Stewart was the one who reacted first. 'She's right. That's the only way up here. We need to block it.'

That was it. They were all moving. John Wayne and Gary Cooper hurled a table. Clark Gable led two other actors I recognised but couldn't name to throw another. Table after table went onto the stairs, a heavy barricade of metal, wood and broken glass.

'It will slow them but not stop them,' Erimem said.

I looked across to the bar where a bartender was shouting into the receiver. 'I think the cops are on their way.'

'They may not be quick enough,' Erimem answered.

She was right. The ledges to the side of the stairs weren't completely blocked. Zombie arms were starting to claw at the ledges.

Erimem looked at a chair for a second then smashed it against the wall with all her strength. It shattered but the legs looked like they would make solid clubs. She tossed one to me and one to Helena. Ibrahim was smashing another chair so Erimem kept two clubs for herself. When she fought she usually liked a weapon in either hand for balance.

The first Nazi zombie head appeared above the ledge.

Erimem swung hard and caught the zombie across the face, sending it backwards. Another zombie got the same treatment from her. I dealt with the next one.

Ibrahim and Helena had dealt with a couple trying to clamber up the other side.

There were a lot of them. Too many. They were trying to scramble up in numbers. They didn't care what damage they were doing to themselves. They just wanted to get at *us*.

'Is there another way out of here?' Erimem shouted. 'A rear entrance?'

I brought my makeshift club down on a zombie's head. 'Think we can get out that way?'

Erimem grabbed an actor. 'Find if there is a rear exit and see if it is clear for us to get these people away.'

The actor hurried away.

'You just sent Jimmy Stewart on a reconnaissance mission.'

'Did I?' Erimem smashed another zombie but she had to step backwards. 'There are too many for us to hold back.'

She was right. They were swarming. Blocking the stairs had slowed them but it hadn't stopped them. Duke and a bunch of others were still blocking the stairs with everything they could find but it wouldn't hold them for long.

'How in the hell did we get Nazi zombies?' I asked Erimem.

'I don't know,' she answered, clattering another zombie. 'I suppose they could have used the incantation,' she said thoughtfully, 'but if they used it properly these zimbies...'

'Zombies.'

'...yes, these zombies would be a disciplined, trained army not these animals.' She smacked another one in the skull. It felt like she did it just for emphasis.

That meant the incantation hadn't been recited accurately. 'So somebody who didn't know the incantation properly did a half-arsed job and turned the Nazis into zombies. Bloody epic.'

Erimem sent another zombie flying backwards. 'Swear about it later. We must hold these creatures back.'

Jimmy Stewart ran back to us. We were out of luck. 'They're trying to get in the back door as well. I've blocked the door the best I can. They won't get in that way but it's no way out.'

Erimem looked back at the stairs. 'That is not good news. They are almost through the barricade.'

Jimmy Stewart looked worried. 'I don't know what these fellas have been smokin' but this is going to get bad.'

Erimem planted her shoe in the chest of a zombie and kicked him backwards. 'Mr Stewart, are you suggesting we should step back and let the men handle this?'

Jimmy Stewart shook his head. 'Well, I suppose I probably should but I saw you swing those chair legs so I won't bother.

You don't have a spare there do you?'

Erimem handed across one·of her weapons. 'Swing hard. They will show no mercy. Neither must we.'

They were through.

The first of the zombies pushed past the last of the table and was through. Erimem was on him. I followed her in. She swung low, shattering the zombie's knee. I took it on the side of the head.

Two more were already through. More were spilling past on Ibrahim and Helena's side. There was just no way the two of them could hold back so many.

They swarmed at us. I lost track of everybody else. I swung that solid piece of wood and kept swinging it. I punched, I kicked. They were screaming behind us. I didn't care. I had to ignore it.

Keep fighting.

There were so many of them.

Keep fighting.

One broke forward. I kicked its leg out but it caught me and dragged me down. I kicked and punched. It was so damn strong. I couldn't break free. It had me. It was going to kill me. I was going to be one of those things.

It was gone.

It was staggering in front on me. A huge right hand smashed into its face, putting it down. Duke pulled me upright. 'You all right?'

'Thanks for the help.'

'Keep fighting, sister.'

He was back into it, swinging fists and slugging zombies. Clark Gable was the same. Gary Cooper waded into the middle of it. Jesus, so did Bette Davis. Everybody was fighting for their lives. Women who were screaming wimps in their movies fought like animals, battering zombies with bottles, chairs and anything else that came to hand. We lost some, but we were holding our own.

Helena and Ibrahim fought their way to me. Ibrahim was cut but he was okay.

'We can't hold them,' Helena said. 'There are too many of them.'

'They're at the back door as well so there's no way out that way,' I answered.'

Erimem spun past and kicked one of the zombies in the balls. Nothing happened. I twatted it in the head with my club and it went down.

Erimem looked as worried as the rest of us. 'I don't know how we can win,' she admitted.

Another voice, somebody we'd forgotten in the battle. 'Stone?'

We turned to Lisa Borden. 'What?'

She pointed to the ledge at the side of the stairs. A familiar face was clambering over. He was deathly pale with blood coming from his mouth.

Detective Stone.

And he was a zombie.

Erimem didn't hesitate. She pulled her club back and swung.

CHAPTER FIFTEEN

Jesus H Christmas.

All I saw was what looked like a wooden table leg flying for my skull. I fought to get here and that was how I was going to go?

A second chair leg deflected the one flying at my skull. Queenie looked angry and surprised. She had been trying to brain me. Her agent was the one who had saved my head.

'He's not dead,' Helena said. 'He's hurt but he's not dead.'

Queenie wasn't convinced. 'Are you sure?'

'How long have I been a doctor?' Helena sounded pissed about being doubted.

Me? I was just excited I'd found a medic. 'Hey, you're a doctor?' My voice sounded pathetic and weak, even to me. 'I gotta tell you, I don't feel too good.'

The guy, Ibrahim, pulled me up. I was glad for the help. I didn't have the energy to get myself upright. Hell, I didn't have the energy for anything. 'Thanks.'

'Stone.'

I got hit by a flying missile named Lisa Borden. She just grabbed me and held on tight. I didn't even have the strength to hug her back.

'I thought you were dead,' she said.

'Sorry to disappoint you,' I answered. My knees finally buckled. 'I think I am.' I coughed up more blood. Hell of a way to make a point.

'Stone! Stone?'

The older woman, Doctor Helena, was at my side, looking in my eyes, checking my pulse. In the middle of a battle with the walking dead she was giving me a physical.

'He needs a hospital,' she said. 'Right now.'

Some doctor. Even I knew I needed a hospital.

'Hide him in the office where Helena tended Lisa,' Queenie said.

'There's no way out from there.' I don't know who the hell said that. I was having trouble focusing. I think I was hallucinating. I must have been. Otherwise I saw John Wayne, Clark Gable and Humphrey Bogart duking it out with these monsters.

'Anybody got a bright idea for how we get out of here?' Lisa asked. She had a nice voice. She'd even forgiven me for killing her.

Bright.

Why was "bright" sounding in my head?

'Bright,' I said. 'Bright lights stop them.'

'Are you sure?' That was Queenie.

'Of course he is.' You know, I think I like that Lisa Borden. She stuck up for me there.

'Okay.' Queenie was looking at the roof. 'Where are the brightest lights?'

My doctor lady pointed at the spot lights at the back of the room. 'The spotlights.'

The cute sister pointed at the mirror-ball hanging from the ceiling. 'If we can hit the light off that it'll go in all directions. We can hit a dozen at once.'

They were gone.

Damn, I hadn't been hallucinating. The Duke really was throwing haymakers at the walking dead. Bogey... I always knew he'd be a dirty fighter.

Queenie and her sister were running. One of the Nazis got in the way. It was Gut-Shot. How come he looked healthier than me? Queenie cracked her baton across his knees. Her sister slugged him in the gut with her club. He dropped. They've got class those dames. They used him as a stool to get up on the bar. The dead clawed at them. They just kicked the dead in the teeth and kept running. When they ran out of bar they kept going. They leaped over the heads of Basil Rathbone and Errol Flynn. You know, Flynn fights better with a sword.

Queenie and her sister made it to the lights and turned those suckers on, full power.

They swung the lights around the club. One caught the mirrorball sending beans of lights all across the room.

The effect was like flicking a switch. The dead guys staggered back, covered their faces, dropped to their knees. The more light hit them, the worse they were affected. They lost control, covered their eyes, dropped to their knees. Some shook out of control. Others looked dead. A few just tried to run. The lights caught up with them and they went down.

We had won.

I didn't feel like I had won.

Truth is, I didn't feel much of anything.

I knew breathing was getting tough. I was kinda struggling to focus. My arms, my legs. I wanted to move them. Nope. Couldn't feel them. I coughed up more blood.

Lisa looked worried.

I should have been worried too, I guess. I was past that point. Things were fuzzy and I just didn't have the energy to worry.

Lisa Borden was crying.

I didn't want her to cry.

I wanted to see her smile.

Just one more time.

I guessed that wasn't going to happen.

'Time to say...'

I didn't have time to finish. My eyes were too heavy. But yeah, it was time to say goodbye.

CHAPTER SIXTEEN

Lisa Borden's scream cut through everything.

It went from a rabble to near silence.

She was kneeling with Detective Stone's head in her lap.

We were at the farthest end of the club and we could see from her expression what that scream meant.

Stone was dead.

He'd dragged his way across the city to warn us. To warn *her*.

Damn it.

We hurried back to her. Carson Reed tried to talk to us but Erimem brushed him aside.

'Leave us alone!'

Helena was examining Stone when we got there. Lisa refused to let go of him. She cradled his head to her. Helena worked around her.

'Definitely a punctured lung,' Helena said. 'He's lost so much blood and there's internal damage. Even if we could get him to a hospital, there's no way to save him.'

So he wasn't dead *yet*.

But he would be in a few minutes. He had closed his eyes to sleep and he wasn't going to wake up again.

Ibrahim squeezed Helena's hand. He is the quiet one of us. Sometimes I overlook what he does. We'd all have fallen apart a hundred times without him.

I hoped Lisa Borden had somebody she could rely on. She was going to need them.

She had picked up on what Helena had said. 'He's still alive?'

'Only just,' Helena said kindly, 'and it's only a matter of minutes.'

'How can you know?'

'I told you, I'm a doctor?'

'And a movie agent? And a spy?'

Helena met rage and frustration with kindness. 'Above everything, I'm a doctor. I promise you, there's no way I can save him. He's as good as gone now.'

'Are you certain?' Erimem asked. 'He showed great courage to come for his woman with these injuries.'

Lisa's answer automatic. 'I'm not his woman.'

'I guess he thought different,' Helena said.

Lisa looked at the still face in her lap. 'Yeah.'

Helena had thought of something. Or at least she was thinking of something. You get to know the expressions people wear. She was definitely running something through her head. She looked from Stone to the zombies back to Stone. 'Those things are dead, right?'

'Yes,' Erimem agreed.

Helena pushed on. 'But are they *actually* dead? They're still moving.'

Ibrahim answered, 'In a fashion. It's more reacting than moving.'

I kind of saw where Helena was going. 'But... that does mean they're still breathing.'

Helena agreed. 'If we all dismiss hocus-pocus mysticism and accept that there's a scientific rationale something in that condition is keeping even those with the worst injuries alive. Could we use that?'

Erimem's head tilted and she frowned. 'Are you saying we should turn him into a zombie?'

'No,' Helena answered quickly. 'Well, a bit.'

'No,' Erimem said immediately.

Don't argue with Helena when she's being a doctor. She doesn't give up. 'Only enough to keep him alive till we get him to a hospital and repair the damage done to him.'

'And then we have what?' Ibrahim asked. 'A healthy zombie?'

'And how do we cure him?' Erimem added.

Helena searched for a pulse in Stone's neck. 'One crisis at a time.'

'You don't know?' Lisa Borden asked.

'Curing zombies isn't exactly in the training manual.'

It was more than just a medical question. I wondered if history had the answer. 'Erimem, this is your history. You knew of the statue and the incantation. Do you know how to cure him?'

'No... but I remember how the undead were defeated.'

That was promising. 'How?'

'They were burned.'

'Shit,' I said. 'The only way to save him is to turn him into a zombie and burn him?'

'Pardon me if I don't know what to do,' Helena snapped.

Erimem had made a decision. 'Infect him.'

Ibrahim wasn't convinced. 'Erimem, I don't know...'

She interrupted, 'Helena, will he die if you don't?'

'Yes.'

'Then is there any alternative?'

'He might be better off dead than turned into whatever one of them is,' Ibrahim said.

It was a hellish situation. There wasn't a right or a wrong answer. We couldn't know what the best option was.

'Very well.' Erimem turned to Lisa. 'He is your man, you must choose.'

'He's not my guy,' Lisa protested again. Even she didn't sound convinced. 'What are my options? To let him die or you turn him into one of those things to save him?'

'Hopefully turn him temporarily,' Helena confirmed.

Lisa nodded. 'Do it. If there's a chance of saving him, do it.'

That was all Erimem needed to hear. She turned to Helena. 'All right. How will you do it?'

'You think I've thought that far ahead?'

'How are illnesses usually passed?' Erimem asked.

'Blood, saliva, bodily fluids, sneezes...'

I shook my head. 'We didn't see any of those happening.'

You could see Helena's brain churning through what she knew. 'Touch? No, if it was touch we'd all be changing. So would half of Hollywood after that punch-up.'

I thought about everything we had seen as the zombies attacked. 'We saw a kind of energy crackle, right?'

Helena nodded. 'So it was an energy transfer?' She thought for a moment. 'Okay. I'm going to need one of the zombies.'

We hurried over and looked for a zombie that wasn't hurt too badly. We found one that was glazed over and not moving.

'Careful.' Duke hurried across. 'We don't know how long they'll be out.'

'We need one that's still twitching,' I told him. He didn't look too happy with that.

'What the hell for?'

'To save somebody's life.'

That was enough for him. 'This one.' Duke dragged the zombie across by the ankle. Helena had already yanked the wires free from a table lamp. She attacked a second wire with a bare end to Stone's chest and then did the same to the zombie with the other end.

She wasn't confident. 'This might work, it might not.' She looked around to make sure we were all ready. 'If it does work, hold them both down.'

Erimem moved closer.

'Not now,' Helena warned. 'If you're touching him when I zap him you'll be zombified as well. Stand back.

She pushed the plug into the socket. The zombie jerked to life. She quickly yanked the plug from the socket.

The zombie tried to sit up. 'It's alive,' Ibrahim warned.

'Not for long.' Duke whacked the zombie. The dead were dead to the world again.

Stone wasn't. He was jerking violently. We all leaped on him to pin him down while Helena gave as much of an examination as she could.

'His heartbeat is still slow and he's barely breathing – but he's breathing.'

Ibrahim tried to grab his legs without much success. 'Tell him that. He's kicking like a mule.'

I grabbed a couple of lamps and tore the wires free. We used them to tie Stone's hands and feet. We wrapped him in a couple of discarded table cloths to make a makeshift stretcher and we carried him towards the door.

'I hope you know what you're doing,' Ibrahim said.

Helena gave a nod of agreement. 'So do I.'

Erimem caught Helena's arm. At the same time she put out a hand to stop me. 'Can you take them to the hospital?' she asked Helena.

Helena looked confused. 'What about you two?'

'We have to stay here.'

'Why?'

'The statue,' Erimem said. 'We must find it.'

I nodded at the zombies. 'And we have to do something about Night of the Living Dead here.'

Helena agreed. 'If the police take them it'll be awkward.'

'That'll be *awkward*?' Carson Reed choked.

'It'll be bad publicity, Carson,' Helena said. 'Nobody's going to believe this.'

The poor git looked shell-shocked. 'Aren't they?'

'You know they're just going to say it's Hollywood out of control or a bunch of reefer addicts.'

'That'd be bad news,' I agreed, 'and our pictures will be associated with it.

The threat to business was like a slap in the face for Carson. He pointed at the zombies. 'What do I do with all of these?'

'Lock them up,' Erimem said.

'Where?'

I gave him a push. 'You're the producer. Produce something.'

Erimem caught his arm. 'But before you do, we need to be make sure none of them have the statue.'

It turned out none of them had the bird but we did find addresses on some of them. We – okay, make that a waitress we collared - used them to create a sort of path for the march of the zombies.

Erimem and I followed the instructions we'd been given by the waitress. There were signs of attacks all the way. Cops were talking to people who had witnessed... something they couldn't explain. Ambulances picked up those who had been attacked and not turned.

We kept our heads low and kept moving.

You get a feeling for some things after a while. When you've seen danger, you get a sense of it. A Spidey-sense.

We had moved into the rough part of town. It was mostly abandoned.

It didn't take long to find the place we were looking for. An abandoned motel in a crud part of town. The sick green and purple light glowing out of shattered windows was a giveaway.

We weren't the first to find the place either.

A bunch of hoods were getting out of a car. The scars on their faces and guns under their arms said this wasn't a choir practice.

'More Nazis?' Erimem asked.

'Nazis? I hate these guys.'

She gave me the look. I guess it wasn't time for an *Indiana Jones* reference. I'm glad she got it, though.

She pointed at the glowing windows. 'The statue must be active. We cannot let these men have it.'

'What happens if they do get it?'

'We will have another zombie army to fight.'

One zombie army in a day is bad luck. Two is just ridiculous. 'How do we stop them?'

'We fight until they fall or we do.'

'We're outnumbered two to one and they have guns. We don't.'

'They are men. We are warriors.'

I hoped the dialogue in her movie was better than that cheese. It was too late to argue. She was already running for the building with the green and purple windows.

I went through the door two steps behind her. Two of the thugs had reached the landing. Two were still on the stairs. Erimem took the stairs three at a time. She caught one guy by the back of his collar and pulled hard. He toppled backwards and rolled down the stairs. I had to jump so he could pass under me. By the time I landed, Thug Number Two was on his knees, clutching the bannister to stop himself from following his friend face first down the stairs. I gave him a knee to the face as I passed. Erimem moved the way she always did in battle. She was fast, spinning, constantly turning and lashing out hands and feet in precise, vicious movements. One blow took the third goon on the side of the head and bounced his skull off a doorframe. The last of the four was more ready for the coming attack than any of the others. He didn't have any qualms about throwing haymakers at a woman either. Erimem dropped to a knee under a wide swinging right hook and she slammed a punch into his nuts. She was on her feet again in a blink and knocked the thug on his arse. The back of his head hit the floor hard.

Erimem didn't slow. 'Hurry,' she said, hurrying towards a doorway gleaming purple and green.

At the door we looked inside. The statue stood on a scabby old table. Light glowed from its eyes and beak and shone from all the carved lines and markings. Papers were scattered on the table.

'Is it safe to go in?' I asked.

Erimem gave a sort of shrug. 'How would I know?'

We moved in carefully. Erimem didn't touch the statue itself but she did pick up the papers.

She scanned the sheets of paper. 'I know these words.'

'What are they?'

'The incantation to raise the dead. This is the...' she stopped. 'No, these words are not correct.'

'I looked at the hard-written words at the bottom. I recognised them and straight away it clicked from where. 'The Blues Brothers?'

'The Blues Brothers?'

'A movie,' I explained. 'These last words are the lyrics – well, kind of lyrics – from a song, Minnie the Moocher. Somebody sabotaged the incantation with the Blues Brothers.'

Erimem sighed in exasperation. 'And in doing so set the dead walking out of control. There was enough of the incantation to raise them but not to put them under anyone's command.'

'That's a bugger.' I'm good with understatement.

'Yes,' she agreed. 'Bugger.'

'So what do we do?'

'I must use a different incantation to kill the statue.'

'Do you know the incantation?' I asked.

She winced. 'I'm not certain.'

'You're not certain?

'It is a long time since I was told of these rituals,' she answered. 'At the time I thought they were silly. Shemek told me

I should pay more attention.'

'Do you think you can remember the incantation to power it down?'

'I will try.' She didn't sound convincing.

'Good.'

One of the goons groaned and staggered to his feet. He lurched towards the room. Erimem slammed the door into his face. We heard him collapse outside. 'Oops.'

'Yeah, right. Oops.'

'I will try the incantations.' She nodded at the door. 'You will need to keep these men from interrupting me.'

'I guess you don't mean by singing.'

She looked around the room, grabbed an old walking stick from the side of the fire and tossed it to me. 'That is the best we have.' She nodded at the door. 'Keep them busy while I try to remember the words.

'What happens if you get the words wrong?'

Her mouth quirked in a sort of shrug. 'Things get worse.'

'How can they get worse than Zombie Nazis?'

The guy outside of the door tried to stand up. I smacked him with the walking stick. 'All right,' I told Erimem, 'get on with it.'

I heard her beginning a chant. I didn't have time to pay attention. The thugs were getting back to their feet.

Erimem had called us both warriors. She was wrong. *She* was a warrior. I was her mate and she had showed me how to fight. How to defend myself. That didn't make me a warrior.

But the idea of more living dead gave me the strength to fight.

The nearest thug reached into his jacket for a pistol. I brought the stick down across his arm. A second later his scream replaced the crack of his arm breaking.

The one who had gone face first down the stairs was dragging himself towards the landing. He pulled at the one I had kneed in the head.

They both looked pissed. Injured but pissed. They were both bleeding. My knee had cost one a couple of teeth. He was going to want payback for that.

'Damn bitch.'

He didn't sound German. He was American. American

Nazis? Didn't we have enough of them in 2018?
I didn't have time to worry.
All I could do was swing my fists.

CHAPTER SEVENTEEN

Dying was supposed to be peaceful.

That's what they always say right?

Everything goes dark then a golden light takes us to the hereafter.

I was kinda ready for that. I'd been noble. I'd done the right thing. At least as far as I could tell. Yeah. Dead with my chin held high and my head in Lisa Borden's lap.

Lisa Borden.

These people would look after her. They were British agents, right?

I felt the darkness, felt the cold.

I was going.

A few minutes and I'd know if there was anything after this life. I'd know more than the smartest scientists or the Pope himself.

I was okay with it.

Was it too late to turn Catholic? Just in case there really was a god?

Hey, they were right. There really was a bright light.

And, Jesus, it hurt.

Hard purple and green light, burning my brain.

So bright, so painful.

I wanted to scream. I couldn't.

I wanted... I wanted...

The urge hit me hard. It filled my mind. It was all I could think. It was the only thing that mattered.

I wanted to fight to be free. I had to lash out, to fight.

Why couldn't I move? I was pinned down, held down.

I was a captive. Captured.

There were lights. Bright lights. They hurt my eyes. The pain made me angry. More than angry. It was rage and I couldn't control it.

I wanted to fight. I had to fight. Needed to fight.

I didn't care who I would fight. I just needed to lash out.

Why? I didn't care.

The North African guy was there. The attractive dark haired woman. British? I recognized them, couldn't remember where from. I should like them. I felt that. They looked worried. They were talking to me. At me.

I didn't care. I didn't want to hear what they were saying. I just wanted to fight. I wanted to hurt them.

I needed to lash out. Anger made me need to let that violence out. I needed to fight and kill.

A blonde woman tried to calm me. That made me angrier.

Hit her. Hurt her.

Her face. I knew her face. I wanted to tear it from her.

I wanted to protect her.

I wanted to kill her.

And then kill everybody else in my way.

She was speaking. I should have understood what she was saying. I should have recognized the words.

I didn't.

That's not right. I recognized the words. I just couldn't understand them. Something stopped me making sense of them.

I didn't care.

I just needed to lash out. Nothing else mattered.

Somewhere inside I knew that I should worry about that blonde woman.

Part of me was confused. Most of me didn't care.

The part of me that did care wanted her to be safe. It said I had to protect her. Why should I protect her? I didn't know who she was.

I didn't know who *I* was.

And it didn't matter.

Something hard hit me. In the brain.

Desperation.

I knew what I had to do.

I needed others like me. I had to *make* others like me. That was why I existed. And then I had to protect... something. It was green and purple. It looked like... a shape I should have recognized but didn't. But I had to protect it. That was what I was *for*.

I pulled at whatever was holding me down. I felt my muscles strain, felt them grow.

The bonds broke.

The three people in the room ran. They dragged the blonde out.

The door couldn't stop me. I was in a hospital. *What was a hospital?* It didn't matter. There were people in beds. I threw myself at them, felt a power flow out of me as I beat them. I felt their bones break under my fists... and I felt them grow stronger.

Three of them, each in a room. Everybody else had run. It didn't matter. We'd get to them all. Nobody could escape from us.

Men in blue were ahead. The word 'police' came into my mind. I didn't know why. They stood in front of us, blocking our way. The female among us – the one with red hair – dragged one to the ground. She smashed her fists into him again and again. The energy passed into him.

The three who ran. They were in front of us as well. The blonde woman. The others were pulling her away. She was crying, saying something. It made no sense.

That desperation hit me again. We *had* to be out of there. We *had* to protect the lights.

The blonde was still trying to talk, still trying to stop me.

I threw myself at her.

CHAPTER EIGHTEEN

I was out of my depth.

Erimem's training put me in decent shape to take on anybody one on one. I could beat the shit out of most muggers.

Four trained thugs were out of my league.

I kicked and punched anything that moved. I kicked at their balls and punched at their throats. One of them dropped clutching at his neck, gurgling.

I could just hear Erimem speaking in ancient Egyptian. There was rhythm and cadence in her speech. She was definitely reciting something. She had tried several versions of the incantation. None had worked.

And I needed one to work. I was losing.

A hard punch on the shoulder sent me reeling. I struggled to regain my balance but one of them was on me, clutching at my throat. I punched him hard. He didn't let go. I pushed the middle knuckle out so it was raised. Erimem had showed us all how to punch this way. 'Aim for the eye,' she had said. 'A blind opponent will not harm you.'

I slammed that knuckle into my attacker's eye. He cried out but didn't let go. He just squeezed harder.

I punched again. Again. Again.

I hit him with everything I had.

I was weakening. Couldn't breathe, couldn't fight. I didn't have the strength.

Darkness was coming fast. It was on the edge of my vision, spreading for the centre. I was done. I had nothing left. No energy.

This wasn't how I thought I'd die.

So anticlimactic.

There was no struggle left.

Just darkness.

I was done.

I woke up, gasping.

Erimem was looking at me. She was as close to panic as I'd ever seen her.

'Andy? Are you all right? Can you speak?'

My throat ached viciously. 'I'm okay.' I sounded like... well, I sounded like somebody had tried to strangle me.

The four thugs all lay on the landing. They were all showing signs of having pissed Erimem off. The one who had tried to strangle me would be in hospital for a while. The others would all need a trip to whatever A&E was called in this period.

She hugged me tight. A hug never felt better, I promise you. Then she was gone. She grabbed one and slapped him until he was awake. 'Who sent you? Who sent you here?'

He was barely conscious but still managed to refuse to reply in just the wrong way. Thirty seconds later he was squealing like a pig and telling us everything we wanted to know. Erimem's hardly more than five feet tall and she can look like butter wouldn't melt in her mouth.

She also has no problems with torturing her enemies to get answers.

She pulled me to my feet. 'We must go.'

'Did you stop it?' I didn't see any flashing green and purple.

'Yes.' She led me towards the stairs. She has the statue in one hand. 'I have this. I also burned the words that were written.'

'So we can go?' You can bet your ass I wanted out of there.

'We *must* go,' Erimem answered. 'I need to get the statue to safety. After we go to the hospital.'

When we arrived at the hospital there was screaming. People were running out the large doors at the front. Even the cops were running.

Yeah, we were in the right place.

We found Helen and Ibrahim inside. They both had blood smeared on their faces and clothes.

Lisa Borden sat on the floor, cradling Stone's head in her lap.

I couldn't tell from anybody's expression whether infecting Stone had kept him alive or not.

It didn't look good.

CHAPTER NINETEEN

Everything hurt.

And it hurt bad.

Opening my eyes wasn't my smartest idea. I winced but stuck with it. The last real memory I had before the crazy dreams were that I was dying.

Unless the hereafter was a real disappointment and looked like a hospital room, I guessed I had survived.

'You're alive.' A nurse was standing by my bed. She looked pissed.

'Yeah, sorry about that.'

'You have other things to be sorry about.'

I didn't like the sound of that. I was glad that she left.

That was when I saw the other figure in the room. A woman sitting in a chair in the darkest corner of the room. Her blonde hair looked yellow as it reflected the streetlight from outside.

I wondered how long Lisa Borden had been sitting there. I wondered how long I had actually been there. I was aching and I could feel bandages around me.

Lisa was quiet. She didn't move. I thought she was asleep until she spoke. 'Stone?'

'Yeah?'

'Is it really you?'

'Who else would I be?'

'Not who,' she answered. '*What*.'

'I don't understand.'

'No, they said you wouldn't.' She stood and crossed to my

bed. 'You don't remember, do you?'

'Remember what?' I asked.

She moved a little closer. Her arm was in a sling.

A memory came out of my nightmare.

It was me leaping at Lisa Borden, gripping her arm tightly.

'Oh, god, no.'

I couldn't look at her. I didn't dare. I'd attacked her. It was me who had injured her arm. I remembered. I'd wanted to kill her. I'd wanted to hurt her.

I squeezed my eyes tightly shut. I just couldn't bear to see her. I couldn't look at the way I'd hurt her.

'How do you feel?' she asked.

It was a simple damn question. I didn't know how to answer. I didn't know how to speak to her.

'I know you can speak, Stone. Before we talked I heard you tell Attila the Nurse to go to hell.'

What the hell could I say? How could words make up for what I did? 'I'm sorry. Lisa, I'm sorry.'

She looked at the sling. 'For the arm? So am I. I won't be using it for a few days.'

'I don't know what to say.'

'You could try saying sorry again.'

'I'm sorry.'

'Or you could say it wasn't your fault.'

It *was* my fault. I remembered doing it. I remembered her screaming. 'I can't.'

'Sure you can.' She sounded hard, assertive. 'If this was anybody's fault it was mine.'

'No.'

She wouldn't let me talk. 'Shut up, Stone. Whatever happened to you, I was the one who decided you should be infected. I made that call.'

That didn't make any sense. 'Why?'

'It was the only way to keep you alive.'

That didn't make any sense either. 'By turning me into... well, whatever I was?'

'It worked. You're alive, aren't you?'

'Am I? Properly alive?' That was what I needed to know. Was I still one of those things?

Lisa reassured me. 'You're pale but you're not green, though you need to stop moving.'

'What?'

'You had surgery. That English woman, Helena... she operated on you.'

'The spy dame?'

Lisa nodded. 'She's a doctor. A good one, too. They say she saved your life.'

'Do they?'

'And she says infecting you with this stuff kept you alive long enough for her to operate on you. It even left something that'll heal you and the others guys quicker than usual.'

I still couldn't forget what I had done. 'It kept me alive long enough to try to kill you.'

'I ain't going anywhere, Stone.'

I turned away. 'You should.'

She still wasn't taking my BS. 'What happens to you if I do?'

'I go back to work.'

'In your office? I looked in there. Looked like you'd had other visitors, too. The place is a mess.'

'It's the cleaning lady's year off.'

She ignored my sass. What will you be doing there? Looking for lost cats? Taking sleazy pictures of women getting a bit of affection away from their husbands?'

I snorted. I shouldn't have. It hurt like hell. 'You make it sound cheap.'

'How often do you eat, Stone?'

'Do ice cubes count as food?'

'I thought so.' Her voice softened. 'You don't eat, you drink too much, you sleep at your office half the time.'

'How do you know that?'

'I told you. I looked in on my way back here.'

'It's not usually that much of a mess.'

'I guessed. I also guessed it wasn't the mice.'

'They left for a better neighborhood.'

'Maybe you should, too.'

She was telling me I could do better, that I could *be* better. God knows I wanted to be.

But the world doesn't run on "want to be", does it?

I answered honestly. 'I think I need to leave town before Mr Gray finds me.'

'The guy who hired you to find the bird?'

I nodded. That hurt, too. 'Yeah, he's gonna be ticked.'

'I guess he is.' She sat on the side of my bed. 'You need somebody to look after you, Stone.'

I snorted. 'I've needed that for years.'

'When was the last time you had somebody offering to take the job?' She took my hand.

It took a minute to get what she was saying. 'Lisa?'

'You didn't kill me, Stone. When the others beat people half to death, you held back from hitting me. Instead, there's a wall outside with holes in it the size of your fists.' She tapped her sling. 'Apart from this, I'm okay. You couldn't hurt me. You couldn't do it.'

I shook my head. 'I don't remember that.'

'I'm not surprised. Ibrahim brained you pretty hard.'

'I guess I have to thank him for that,' I said sourly.

'I guess you do.'

This was crazy. We had to be real. 'Lisa, we hardly know each other.'

'I know.'

'And I'm an ass-hole.'

'I know that, too.'

'Thanks.'

'But you're not the worst ass-hole I've met in this town. Somewhere under there is a really good guy.'

I didn't think I could believe that. 'If there is, I haven't seen him in a long time.'

Her hand stroked my face. 'Don't worry. I see him. I'll help you find him.'

'Lisa, this is crazy.'

'Yeah, it is.' She shrugged. 'But this is Hollywood, so what's new in that?'

I didn't have an answer.

I was tired. My eyes were closing. I felt her hand pull away. I held it tighter.

The last thing I felt before I fell asleep was the bed shift as Lisa lay down beside me.

CHAPTER TWENTY

Production on the movie was stopped for two days. Two whole days. We did that.

When Erimem shut the Falcon down, the zombies it was controlling dropped. They were puppets with their strings cut. Most of them wound up in hospitals across the city – including our leading lush, John Buttler. Carson Reed fell back on his stand-by excuse.

'It was a party at Errol Flynn's house.'

It's amazing how Hollywood clammed up and covered up when there was a hint of scandal. Most people thought it was drugs. That was easier to sell than zombies.

The press were shut up with promises of interviews with the stars and threats that their opposition would get the scoops for the next decade if even a single paper broke ranks. I guess dollar bills trump journalistic integrity.

I need to start using a different word than "trump". Just saying it makes me feel ill.

So, we had a couple of days off. For those two days we tied up loose ends.

The first one was Stone's boss. Mr Gray. We met him in Cleary's Bar. He might as well have had a neon sign over his head saying ALIEN.

He didn't look comfortable sitting opposite Erimem and Helena. He was even less comfortable when Ibrahim and I brought chairs blocking him in the booth,

'Mr Stone is unable to be present at the meeting,' Helena

said. She had been practicing that agent patter. 'We are here in his place.'

'Are you his subordinates?' Stone's voice was so dead I almost dozed off from one question.

'No,' Helena answered, 'his associates.'

'Do you have my artefact?' Still no tone in that grey voice.

'It's not *your* artefact, though, is it?' Erimem asked. 'It is the property of the royal line of Egypt.'

'Sadly, they are all long gone to dust.'

Erimem glanced at Ibrahim quickly. 'I think we are remarkably well preserved for those gone to dust.'

Gray frowned.

Erimem leaned forward. 'You are not of this world, Mr Gray. I am not of this time. I reigned in Egypt when the pyramids were new and still shone white with plaster. I was Pharaoh of the Two Kingdoms. I led my armies in battle and I slew my enemies. I turned the desert red with their blood and slept soundly afterwards without a nightmare to trouble me.' She held his gaze. 'The Falcon is gone, taken back in time to a point at which it will be found and then make its way here. It is now part of a loop in time. It never goes beyond this point in time. You will never have it.'

Still no emotion from Gray. 'This will cause me great difficulty. That artefact was part of a piece of blood technology created half a million years ago. I have a client who has already paid me a large fee in advance for recovering the statue.'

'Why would anyone want that statue?' Helena asked mildly. 'All it can do is control the dead or indeed the living and turn them into a zombie army.'

'I never ask my clients personal questions,' Gray said in that flat tone. It had stopped being dull. It was sinister now.

'You should ask,' Erimem said coldly, 'and you should choose your clients more carefully.'

'Perhaps I should offer him a time traveller instead of the artefact?'

Well, there was a threat.

Dumb move.

Erimem slowly placed one of her fighting daggers on the table. 'If you repeat that or try to act on it, I will cut the tongue from your mouth, the heart from your breast and then ensure that you are never again in the position to father children. I will gut you and let the jackals feast as you scream your final breath.' She nodded once. 'You will leave this world and never come back. If you return I will know and I will kill you. I swear this on the blood of my line, past, present and future.' She paused, just a heartbeat. 'I will kill you,' she repeated slowly.

Gray showed a speck of emotion for the first time. A slight tremble in his face. He was terrified. He took a minute to answer.

'Very well,' he said quietly. 'I think I must have followed a false trail to this world.'

'I think you must,' Erimem agreed.'

Gray slid out of the booth. I'm pretty sure he actually *slid* or *oozed*. He paused at the door and looked back. Erimem's hand was still on the dagger.

He left.

Our second port of call was nicer surroundings but I was a lot less comfortable.

Some local villain named the Dutchman worked out of the club. He sat like Don Corleone. He didn't like us. He had good reason.

'Two of the men you sent to trail the Detective Stone are dead,' Erimem said.

The Dutchman didn't like that. 'How did they die? Did you kill them?'

'Yes,' Erimem answered. 'They were driven mad by the infection. I had no alternative.'

The Dutchman's eyebrow rose. He knew more than he should. 'Infection?'

'Can you think of a better word?' Erimem answered.

That was a fair point. We had called it a dozen different things and we had no idea what we should call it. In the end we'd settled on "infection".

Dutchie grimaced. 'I don't suppose it matters. What of the Nazis?'

'Dead,' Erimem answered. 'Even after the infection, two died from loss of blood from Stone's bullets. The others... they died in the attack on the club. We killed them.'

The Dutchman was thoughtful, mulling that news. 'Two of my less useful lackeys in return for four dead Nazies? That is a fair trade.' He reached into his drawer and pulled out a bottle of whisky. The good stiff. 'I owe Stone a Scotch. Tell him this is waiting for him.'

Erimem nodded agreement. 'I have one question for you. Did you send those men to kill the Nazis, to help Stone or to steal the statue?'

'Or all of those?' the Dutchman answered.

'Then I will tell you as I have told others,' Erimem said calmly. 'The statue is gone. It is no longer in this country. It is in a safe place.'

'You sent it back to England?' the Dutchman asked. 'By plane?'

'It is no longer in this country,' Erimem repeated. 'It is safe.'

The Dutchman's head tilted to the side. He didn't look too bothered. 'I don't know how I'd make a profit from it anyway.'

'Are *we* safe?' Erimem asked. 'We killed two of your men and injured two others. Are you intent on revenge?'

'If I am?'

'Many people will die. Including you.'

The Dutchman raised his hands. 'The Nazis are dead. That's good enough for me. And you killed a couple... that gets you a free drink in my place.' He looked at the human mountain standing at the door. 'But not today. My boys might need a day to cool off about their friends dying.'

That was fair enough.

We left quickly. I was kind of keen to go home. I was in the mood for chips. And rain. Damn, I missed rain. Proper cold London rain.

Pity we'd have to finish the film before I saw any.

CHAPTER TWENTY ONE

I'd never been invited to a movie premiere before. I guessed this wasn't a big picture. The premiere wasn't grand by Hollywood standards. Centurion were cheap bastards. They must have either had a free bar or held markers on some big names. Wayne, Stewart, Cooper, deHavilland... They all turned up and put on smiles and pretended this wasn't a cheap cheesefest. They had their pictures taken for the papers. Most of them posed with the sisters. I wasn't surprised. They were on the way up, those two.

They could also kill you without breaking a sweat. If they told me I was having my picture taken I'd have agreed.

I did the sensible thing at the premiere. I hit the bar. Pity I was stuck to tomato juice.

'Bloody Mary?' Sister Andy asked. 'Or just sodding tomato juice?'

'Is that an English joke?'

Queenie Erimem appeared by her sister. 'I don't think we can blame the English for this. Andy just has a very strange sense of humour,'

'Not Andy anymore.' Ibrahim had arrived with Doctor Helena, my savior. 'Crystal Smith.'

'Crystal,' Andy snorted. 'I sound like a bloody chav or something from TOWIE.'

Nope. I had no damn idea what a chav or TOWIE were. I didn't ask either.

'I'm surprised you invited us,' I said. 'I haven't seen you in months.'

Helena nodded but she was a little evasive. I still have a nose for that. 'We've been busy since filming wrapped. How about you? Are you recovered?'

I winced a little. It was an instinct. Memory made me do it. I'd spent weeks gasping with every move. It had finally passed thankfully. 'Pretty much,' I answered.

'Are you busy?' the Warrior Queen asked. She looked every inch a movie star. My eyes were elsewhere.

Lisa Stone smiled at familiar faces and eased close to my side. Her arm went around my waist.

'Hi,' she said.

'Hi.'

'Are you keeping him out of trouble?' Helena asked.

'He's head of security ay Centurion now,' Lisa said. I grew a foot taller when I heard how proud she sounded. 'He deals with trouble every day.'

'Little troubles,' I said. 'Actors who forgot where they parked, keeping the public away. That kind of thing. Nothing big.' That made Lisa happier. She liked as little trouble as possible.

Helena scratched her nose. 'Got to say, I'm disappointed we didn't get an invite to the wedding.'

Andy nodded. 'It's not as if any of us saved your life. Oh, wait a minute...'

'It's was quiet,' I apologized. 'We only had Lisa's folks and Red there…'

'Stop teasing them,' Ibrahim said. Helena wrinkled her nose at him. God, they were in love. Why hadn't I noticed that before?

Doctor Helena smiled and held up her bag. Queen Erimem lifted an envelope from it.

'This is our gift to you,' the Queen said. 'Actually it is something we owe you.'

I took the envelope, looked inside and almost dropped it. I handed it to Lisa.

'Five thousand,' Helena said. 'As agreed.'

'We can't,' I said. 'We didn't give you the bird.'

Helena shrugged. 'But we got it anyway.'

'And it is safe,' Queenie added.

Helena was serious. 'So take the money. Buy a house.'

The idea appealed to Lisa. 'We could move out of my parents' place...'

Lisa had moved me in as soon as I got out of hospital so she could watch me recuperate. We were looking for somewhere we could afford and we just hadn't around to moving out yet, even after we were married.

I've got no problem with Lisa's folks. Except for the praying and the church-going and the hectoring that I should go to church... and the insinuation that I wanted to be alone with their daughter all the time. Well, they had me on that one.

Five grand would let us buy a nice place. We both had decent salaries coming in. We'd be more than comfortable.

We'd be *happy*.

I had never expected that would be in my future.

'Thanks,' I said. 'When we move in to the house, we *will* invite you all over then.'

Helena raised a glass. 'You're on.'

'May we borrow your husband, please, Lisa?' asked the Queen. She took one of my arms. Andy – or Crystal – took the other.

'One more gift... we would like you to meet our friend, Duke. He heard you were a fan of his.'

Duke? Wayne? Me?

'Hey,' I heard Lisa's voice from behind us. 'I don't suppose you could introduce me to Errol Flynn?'

'No,' I said, 'they can't.'

Helena and Ibrahim followed.

'This is Hollywood,' Doctor Helena said, 'anything can happen in Hollywood.'

Warrior Queen of the Nile

Egyptian adventure to make a killing at the box office

by Showbiz Correspondent Lola Levesque, the voice of Tinseltown.

Centurion Pictures' latest release, *Warrior Queen of the Nile*, is a rip-roaring adventure mixing the action of *King Solomon's Mines* with the Egyptian mysticism of *The Mummy*. Centurion's favourite leading man John Buttler brings his usual effortless charm to his role as an adventuring archaeologist, displaying Egyptian artefacts in London.

One of the silver screen's most reliable leading men, Buttler forms a strong father-son relationship with young Peter Arthur, who will surely be headlining movies in his own right before long.

The real surprise comes in the athletic performance of newcomer Erimem Smith as the eponymous Queen. She brings a mixture of athleticism and natural charm to her role. She is matched in the glamor stakes by Clementine Reed who gives a winning portrayal as Alice, who may be an ancient Egyptian pricess reborn in the Twentieth Century.

Action, excitement and romance fill the screen in *Warrior Queen of the Nile*.

This issue of **Hollywood Star's** review page is proudly sponsored by Centurion Pictures, the studio you can trust for entertainment.

ERIMEM SMITH... Centurion Pictures' latest action starlet stars in *Warrior Queen of the Nile*.

Hollywood Star, November 1940

WARRIOR QUEEN OF THE NILE
Dir: Carson Reed

Hot on the heels of Universal's horror flicks comes this latest offering from Centurion Studios. Headlined by the reliable John Buttler, *Warrior Queen of the Nile* is directed by Carson Reed.

The action is slick and hard-hitting, the heroes don't take guff from anybody – even from three thousand year old Egyptian priests – and the dames are pretty enough to risk everything fighting for... and in this flick the dames can look after themselves.

It's all hokey stuff but you'll be taken along with the action and you won't realize till later that the Egyptian Queen has an English accent.

This flick owes plenty to film serials and might have played better over fifteen chapters.

Paired with a solid B-pic *Robin Hood's Daughter* you're guaranteed a solid night's entertainment.

January 1941 review, **Hollywood Tattler**

WARRIOR QUEEN OF THE NILE [1940]
Screen Classics
Available for download from July 20th

A bonkers little gem from cheap and cheerful Centurion Studios [the Asylum of their day].

Archaeologist [more like tomb robber] Carlton Franklin, played with gusto by a clearly half-cut John Buttler, is about to unveil his latest discoveries in a museum in foggy London Town. The fog is there to cover up that they never got off of the Centurion lot in LA.

The exhibition attracts the attention of an ancient Egyptian curse and a Cockney criminal gang whose accents make Dick Van Dyke's effort in *Mary Poppins* sound like it came from Guy Ritchie's latest effort.

Things do perk up and the plot goes properly bonkers when an ass-kicking queen from ancient Egypt gets whisked through time to protect her property. Played by newcomer Erimem Smith, who only made three films before disappearing from public life, the warrior queen livens things up enormously, by taking part in regular, very well executed fight scenes. It's clear that the actress did her own stunts and had a blast doing them.

Switch your brain off, enjoy the hokum.

Odd fact: *Warrior Queen of the Nile* is reputed to have been one of John Wayne's favourite films.

Rating ★★★☆☆
A guilty three out of five.

2018 review, www.cheesymovies.ccdn

STUDIO ANNOUNCEMENT

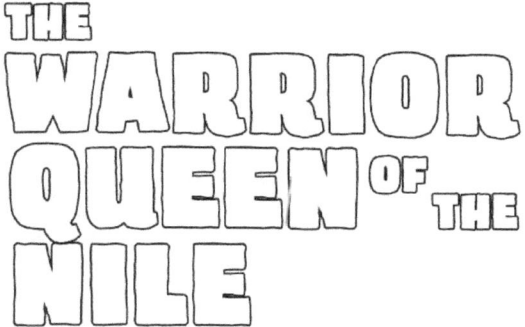

THE WARRIOR QUEEN OF THE NILE

WILL BE BACK IN

THE JEWELS OF CLEOPATRA

COMING SPRING 1941

A Centurion Picture

THE DEATH OF EMPIRE
A novella by Beth Jones

CRY OF THE BRY'HUNEE
A novella by Tim Gambrell

A PHARAOH OF MARS
A novel by Jim Mortimore

www.ingramcontent.com/pod-product-compliance
Lightning Source LLC
Chambersburg PA
CBHW070600180626
46817CB00005B/1919